OFF

THE

PAGE

A Novel

Elizabeth Kenyon

To all the stories I never finished.

ONE

I've always possessed a fifty-fifty success rate when it comes to over-easy eggs.

Don't get me wrong: I'm not ignorant to the fact that more consistent methods exist somewhere on the internet, I've just never looked. Truth is, I live for the suspense. The drama! The elation over a perfectly runny yoke; the defeat of a broken one (or worse, *overcooked*).

I bet Izzie would say the same thing. And Ben would tease her for it.

Today, the breakfast stars have aligned in my favor.

I mash half an avocado on a thick slice of multigrain, sprinkle on some Parmesan cheese, red pepper flakes, S&P, slide my little pride and joy on top, and squeeze some fresh lemon juice to finish—a recipe I totally poached from Common Ground, the coffee shop I work at. Then I kiss my fingertips just for show, even though I'm alone in the kitchen.

The plan was to carry my Millennial Breakfast over to my laptop, boot the old thing up, and try to write, well, *anything*, but, as with most days, that doesn't happen. The reasons vary greatly but the result is always the same.

Today the reason is Suze, my roommate, strolling into the kitchen just as I'm about to leave.

"Oh, *snap*," she says upon spotting my toast. "Wanna make me one?"

That's how we ask for stuff. It's never "can you" or "would you please," but "do you want to" and "how do you feel about." It could very well be a symptom of our passive-aggressive Minnesotan upbringings, but it's more likely because we were friends long before we were ever roommates.

"I was gonna write…" She sticks her bottom lip out in a lame puppy-dog expression. "Ben is waiting for me!" The pout persists. "Fine." She grins. *Sorry, Ben.*

That's when Casey, my other roommate, sticks her head in the kitchen. "What're y'all talkin' about?" Despite the fake inflection, Casey is very much a Northerner. She has the thickest Minnesotan accent out of all of us.

"Avo toast," I reply.

"Ooh! Wanna make me one?"

Sometimes I think making breakfast is the only thing I'm good at.

And even then, it's only fifty-fifty.

Closing shifts are by far the worst of all the shifts. The tips aren't as good as they are in the morning, and it falls on you to do all the cleaning. The one redeeming quality is that you have time to make breakfast in the morning.

Out of my four weekly shifts at Common Ground, only one of them is a closer, and it's by far my least favorite shift. In seven hours, I'll be icing my shoulders in the living room, feet propped up to bring down the swelling. Honest to God, Tuesdays accelerate my body's aging process tenfold. I may not have the science to back my theory, but my muscles don't lie.

At least today, I have the mental clarity of an early rise and a stomach full of avo toast to get me through. That's what I tell myself, anyway, as I tie an apron around my waist, watching on as the openers split their giant pile of cash tips.

The owner, Martha, arrives shortly after I do, several reusable totes in tow.

"Jane, guess what?" She doesn't wait for me to guess. "The store had that fancy oat milk you were talking about last week. We need to make a latte and test it out, stat."

You'd think she'd just met Hugh Jackman, the way she goes on about the oat milk. But then, this is Martha's way. She has a general zest for life that I, nearly thirty years her junior, sometimes envy.

It was with this zest that she acquired Common Ground seven years ago, back when it was a failing coffee shop owned by absent and impersonal entrepreneurs, so she says. When Martha learned through a friend that the place was going up for sale, she immediately knew she had to have it. It had always been a dream of hers to own her own shop, after all. Her husband wasn't as easy to convince, but being a vibrant man himself, he came around eventually.

Common Ground is almost an extension of herself: light and comfortable, with an edge of sophistication. The interior is pleasant to look at, all neutral tones and trendy decorations. The natural light from the corner shop's floor-to-ceiling windows doesn't hurt either.

Martha took a failing business and turned it into one of the most popular spots in Southeast Minneapolis, especially for the MacBook-touting-millennial crowd. On weekends, it's a social spot, though I only ever work during the week. Weekend shifts are fodder for the collegiate employees, something I am not.

No one works more, or harder, than Martha, and when she's not here, she's shopping or planning for the shop. It's rare for a day to go by without her working a shift herself, or popping her head in briefly to see how things are going, or changing a lightbulb, or fixing a leaky faucet. Our regular customers joke that it wouldn't be possible if she didn't have access to coffee 24/7, but the truth is, she doesn't touch the stuff unless it's decaf. She says it's bad for her heart.

The oat milk turns out to be so good, Martha calls up the brand's company to inquire about bulk orders. I sip on the test latte in the small backroom/kitchen/glorified office, and, since we don't get a lot of afternoon traffic, tear into one of the chocolate croissants Martha sources from a local French bakery.

Once we've put all the groceries away, Martha asks if I want her to stay for a bit, just in case we get a push around lunchtime, but I tell her I'm fine. She makes herself a decaf Americano on our gorgeous orange traditional espresso machine—the obvious statement piece in an otherwise neutral-toned environment—before disappearing into the beautiful April afternoon, off to duet with some woodland creatures, probably.

I busy myself with stocking, trying to gauge how busy the morning was by how many cups were used. Looks like they had a good morning.

Then, already bored with this afternoon shift, I sit cross-legged on the floor and begin deep-cleaning the fridge under the traditional. Martha and I are the only ones who ever pull all the milk cartons out to wipe down the very back of the fridge. It's strenuous business, as you have to bend your shoulders at an unnatural angle to successfully reach every nook and cranny, but the result is always satisfying.

Unfortunately, the bell above the door chimes before I get a chance to put everything back.

"Ja-ane!" a familiar voice calls. There's only one person I know who likes to split my name into two syllables.

I pop my head up from below the counter. "Danny P.!"

He rears back dramatically in a rather unconvincing attempt at acting startled. "Why are you on the floor?"

"Cleaning out the fridge. You know how it is."

He does know how it is, though I never once saw him do it himself.

"*Someone's* gotta be the one to do it."

"Funny," I grunt as I place the milk cartons back in an orderly fashion, as well as our famous cold press and iced teas. "You said the same thing when you worked here, too."

I finally stand, using the counter to pull myself up. "What's up?"

"Oh, you know, I just missed Philip." He sidles up to the espresso machine, caressing it softly. "Hey, handsome."

The joke achieves the desired outcome: I laugh loudly.

If laughter were a drug, Daniel Park would be an addict.

Danny was obviously popular in high school; you can just tell those kinds of things. The most glaring evidence of this fact was that he played sports in high school, and his Instagram page has way too many followers despite the fact that most of his photos are four-year-old mirror selfies and soccer action shots. The second most glaring reason is that he was a marketing major.

But that's not even the worst part. The most annoying thing about him is that his popularity is well and truly deserved. Not because of his looks (though being a half-Korean Adonis with soft amber eyes, a light spattering of freckles, and a wide smile doesn't hurt), but because of his killer personality. He's friendly with everyone, generous with his smiles and attention, and genuinely funny. His biggest joy in life is to make people laugh simply so he can laugh with them.

Despite his popularity carrying over into college, which I knew was a thing because of the staggering amount of visitors he would receive on a daily basis at work, he would often send invites to our staff group chat for happy hour meetups, or bonfires on his university campus, even including Martha and her husband.

Unsurprisingly, Danny P. won hearts wherever he went. Developing a crush on him was practically part of the job description.

For me, Danny is what you would call a "near miss." And by that I mean we went out a few times just the two of us, flirted a little, made the occasional meaningful eye contact at work, but never went any further than that.

Truthfully, it's never bothered me much that he never made a move. Danny's a lot of fun, sure, but he has a knack for goofing off even when you don't want him to. Besides, at the time this was all happening, I was focused on a different man, one who took life seriously (sometimes to a fault, Izzie would add).

I know my coworkers thought I was crazy for never taking my chance with Danny. Even Martha once remarked, after Danny had already quit for his fancy marketing job, that we would have looked good together, as if aesthetics alone were a good enough reason to start something.

Despite it all, I'm glad to have Danny in my life in any capacity: coworker, customer, near miss, whatever. He has a talent of making you feel special, like his attention is the sun and sometimes you just want to bask in its warmth.

We still hang out sometimes, especially when he discovers a new bar in the area and needs someone to go with him, extrovert that he is. I'm always surprised when he calls on me to join him, especially when I remember how many Instagram friends he could ask instead, but what can I say, I'm a delight. Plus, I live super close.

"You're going to make me make you avocado toast, aren't you?"

"Yup." He smiles that cursed smile.

I ring him up, using the employee discount even though he hasn't been employed here in over a year. It feels wrong not to; besides, he's here all the time.

I make his drink first while he chatters away about a project he gets to work on at his company. I ask if he wants to try our new oat milk, to which he wholeheartedly consents.

Then, for the third time today, I make avocado toast for someone else.

I sit across from him as he munches away at the toast, an almost exact replica of what I myself ate for breakfast not three hours ago. I tell Danny as much, and he makes a "tsk, tsk" sound with his teeth, as if I'm a common thief for using the recipe at home.

"Whatever. My roommates loved it."

"Mm, Casey and Suze? Do they both still work from home?"

"God, what is your memory. Yeah, they do, believe it or not."
I've returned home on more than one occasion to a tense energy in the apartment, the unsurprising result of two people sharing the same space day in and day out.

"Man, I don't know how they do it. If I sat alone in my apartment every day I think I would shrivel up and die."

"Oh, without a doubt."

Danny finally wipes the crumbs off his lips with a napkin, throwing it down on the plate dramatically when he's done. "*Magnifique*, as always. Unfortunately, I've got to head back to work."

We both rise from the table. I reach for his empty plate, but he scoops it up before I can. "Allow me." He walks it to the backroom quickly and conspiratorially, since he knows he's not supposed to be back there, and sets it, not *in* the sink, but *by* the sink. "There," he says, satisfied with himself. "Now you can wash it."

"Danny P., you are a prince among men."

True to form, my ankles are propped up later that evening in our cozy little living room, a couple of painkillers working their way through my bloodstream.

Our apartment is sandwiched between two popular Minneapolis lakes, a prime location and admittedly way too nice for my paygrade, so I decided as soon as I moved in that I would stay as long as they let me. Our building is charming and old—more on the "old" side, but we have hardwood floors, something Casey and Suze maintain as a blessing.

By some miracle, I'm able to convince Suze to give me a shoulder rub, and she's currently switching between relaxing rubs and painful squeezes.

"Ow!"

"Shhh, the pain means it's working."

"I don't know about that," I mumble.

Casey's sitting in an armchair on her laptop, even though she's already been staring at the screen all day for work. "Case, read a book or something, jeez."

"Your face is a book," she tells me dryly without looking up.

"Your mom is a book," Suze fires back, and I put up my hand for a high-five, which Suze emphatically accepts.

"That doesn't even make any sense," she sighs, but she shuts her laptop anyway, only to pick up her phone instead. "I think I should go blonde." She fiddles with her dark brown strands.

"Then we'd have all three colors!" Suze, a redhead, says.

My hair is also brown, though not as dark as Casey's. Take the token brown crayon from a Crayola box set and you've got my shade. Both lighter in color and less curly than my Middle-Eastern mother's, but just as thick.

Suze slaps down on my shoulders to indicate the conclusion of my massage. "Thanks," I wince.

"Thanks for breakfast." So that's why she was so willing to rub my shoulders. A common exchange of goods and services. *Quid pro quo.* At that, she, too, picks up her phone.

I leave my two roommates to their quiet scrolling sesh and head into dining room, also known as my bedroom.

There's no door to the space, which sits right off the living room, and if it weren't for one of those Japanese folding walls, it would be like I never left the girls.

I don't mind the lack of privacy, especially when I plug my earphones in, which is exactly what I do now as I locate my laptop charger and connect it to the power socket nearest my bed. I climb under the covers and sit up against the wall with nothing but a couple throw pillows between. With my laptop on my lap, I switch it on, fidgeting while it boots up. *Why am I nervous?*

I let out a shaky breath as I glide my fingertip across the mouse pad towards the Word document titled "Untitled." I scroll to where I last left off, nearly six months ago. Even then, I barely managed a chapter.

Guilt swarms my chest as I'm reminded of how I last left them.

Izzie and Benjamin are at something of a standstill, and I have not a clue as to how I can help them.

In the beginning, Izzie can't stand Ben and his stupid handsome face and his neat suits, nor his seemingly systematic approach to life. And Ben can't understand why Izzie applies a laissez fair attitude towards everything but him. He is a man of order; she, a woman of the wind. They were fast enemies.

Until, of course, a series of coincidental events throw them together enough that Ben eventually reveals a hidden human side to him, and Izzie surprises him with deep, philosophical thinking, and they connect despite themselves, leading to a kind of mutual respect—the natural next step in the enemies-to-lovers process.

But the story lacks a certain edge. There's no conflict, not one good enough to act as the much-needed driving force of the story, anyhow, and sometimes it feels like Ben and Izzie's undeniable chemistry gets in the way of actual plot. For months, I tried to come up with some kind of curveball to throw at them, but nothing ever fit the bill. Apparently romantic tension and plucky dialogue is all I'm good for.

I type and delete and retype and re-delete several sentences to no avail before resigning myself to editing old chapters, a big no-no. I read once that you're never supposed to go back and edit until you've finished the rough draft completely, but I commit this transgression all the time.

Perhaps my constant habit to look back instead of ahead is the root of all my problems, but I can't help myself. I keep thinking maybe there's something from the past that I can use to push the story forward—a jumper cable, if you will, for a stalled plot—but I come up with bupkis. Instead, I reword a few sentences and take comfort in words I wrote three years ago, mentally apologizing to Ben and Izzie. Of course, they can't hear me.

Before long, I find myself perusing online shops instead, the rhythmic scrolling making me sleepy. I sink lower and lower into the mattress until sleep finally overtakes me, bringing with it thoughts of Izzie and Ben, vibes and tones and moods, but nothing I can actually work with.

Inspiration strikes the following Tuesday during my short drive to work. But not for my story; no, that would be too good to be true.

Instead, I feel inspired to make soup for dinner, because it's snowing.

We all knew the last few weeks of sunshine were too good to be true. Minnesota's false springs are brutal, and this last push of winter is our burden to bear.

Despite the sleet, I'm in a good mood. It's much easier to be trapped inside at work all day when the world outside is a mess. Plus, there's free coffee.

It's in this frame of mind that I walk into Common Ground for my afternoon shift.

Martha's on the phone when I join her behind the counter, so I utter a quiet greeting as I pass her on my way to the kitchen.

The bell above the door chimes right when I'm in the middle of tying my hair up into a ponytail, so I'm relieved when I hear Martha set the phone on the counter to take their order. It must be her husband on the other line, since she wouldn't put a vendor or a customer on hold like that.

I'm about to join her out front when I spot a couple of dirty dishes sitting in the sink, and since I'm incapable of walking away from a mess, I begin to clean them. It only takes me a minute, and then I'm drying off my hands and leaning on the counter behind the traditional espresso machine, tall enough to obscure the face of the person waiting on their Americano, his head bowed, presumably over his phone.

That's when I notice the phone, still lying face-up on the back counter with the ongoing call. "I can finish up here if you need to get back to that."

"Are you sure?" she asks, as if pressing the button for another shot of espresso is too challenging a task to delegate.

"Yes," I laugh.

She laughs too, as if realizing the silliness of her question. "Thanks." She picks up the phone, disappearing into the kitchen, but not before I hear her address the person on the other line as Jack, her husband. Knew it.

I smile a little to myself, taking an odd sense of satisfaction from the predictability of the shop. How every day, I know what to expect. No surprises. Izzie would hate that, but not me.

Once the espresso has finished pouring into the paper cup, I carry it lidless to the end of the counter, watching it carefully so as not to disrupt the crema.

I smile up at the customer just as I'm setting down the cup.

My eyes suddenly go wide.

"*Ben.*"

TWO

T he name escapes me breathlessly, a statement rather than a question. Because… it's him. I know this face. I've pictured it countless times in my head. *How is this possible?*

I rear back defensively, like I've been hit. Unfortunately, and much to my surprise, I'm still holding tightly to the Americano, and the brash movement sends scalding hot bean water splashing out of the cup and all over my wrist.

"Ah!" I hiss in pain, but thankfully, I don't drop the cup. I set the now half-empty cup down, putting concerted effort into collecting myself.

"I am so sorry," I say—a pretty good start towards redemption, in my opinion—but when I look back up at his unchanged face, whatever normal sentence I planned to impart scatters into oblivion.

"No problem. Are… are you okay?"

What, he *talks*, too?

He's looking at me like I'm deranged. Which, I am, God, I *must* be, to believe my own literary creation has come to life.

"Yeah," I manage to respond, but when I glance down, I notice my wrist has turned an unnatural shade of red. It stings, too.

"Are you sure?" His eyebrows are raised.

"Yes," I say more firmly. "I'll make you a new one right away." I wait a beat, then add, "I don't know what just happened." That, at least, is true.

"Ok," he laughs, wincing sympathetically. *Put your eyebrows down, Benjamin.*

I grind out espresso for his new Americano, focusing way too intently on the process as a means of avoiding his eye. He says nothing more, and I'm grateful for the silence because it gives me a moment to think.

This isn't Ben. It's just someone who looks uncommonly similar, right down to his dark brown eyes. I mean, come on, this was bound to happen eventually. It's not like I gave Ben any unique identifying features. He's Caucasian; classically handsome. There are plenty of guys like him out there. Heck, here's one standing right in front of me.

I successfully set his second Americano down in front of him, squawk out a "thank you," and quickly escape back to the safety of the espresso machine, where I busy myself rinsing out the porta filters.

"By the way, do we know each other?"

His question takes me by surprise, until I remember the first thing I said to him was his name.

A name I've since convinced myself couldn't possibly belong to him.

It can't be...

"Hm?" I play dumb, hoping he'll miraculously forget his question in the next millisecond.

He doesn't let me off the hook. In fact, I feel very much *on* the hook. "Well it's just... you said my name a second ago."

I blanche. *Quick, Jane, say something normal!* "I don't think so."

He looks sideways at me.

"You just, um, look like a Ben."

Stupid!

It's a weird thing to say. I know it, he knows it, the man on the moon knows it, but by the very grace of God, he doesn't press further. In fact, his lips turn downwards humorously, like he's trying to suppress a laugh. Is he enjoying this?

"Okay. Well, thank you for this." He lifts the beverage in his hand. His eyes trail down toward my wrist. "And you're probably going to want to run that under some cold water."

I look down at my poor little wrist, still blazing red.

When I look back up, Ben is already disappearing out the door, the bell signaling that it's time to return to reality.

I dash home as soon as I can, which is pretty easy given I live ten minutes away.

Bursting through the front door, I yell, "Living room, now!" before realizing that both Casey and Suze are already seated in the living room. They look up, alarmed.

"Jane, what's wrong? You've got crazy eyes."

"That's because I am crazy, Casey." I toe off my white sneakers and crash on the plush armchair. "What I'm about to tell you makes zero sense, but I need to tell *someone*." Someone who knows.

They sit up a little straighter. Phones turned off and set aside. Good.

"I met Ben today."

They're obviously confused. "Ben-who?" Suze asks.

"Ben King."

"Ben King… Ben-From-Your-Novel-King?" Casey asks.

"Uh-huh." I've resorted to nail-biting.

Suze narrows her eyes, trying to understand. "Like, someone who looks like what you'd imagined Ben King would look like?"

"Someone who looks *exactly* like what I'd imagined Ben King would look like, and also *has the same name.*"

"First and last?" asks Casey.

"I only confirmed first."

"Okay." Casey sits back in her seat. "So it could just be a wild coincidence."

Even though I came to the very same conclusion, it still doesn't sit right.

"I guess…"

"But you don't believe that." Suze is a sensitive creature. She sees through me immediately.

"I don't know." I bury my face in my hands. "I don't know," I repeat, more to myself.

I'll admit, with every passing hour after my interaction with Ben-Maybe-From-My-Novel-King, the idea that it's anything *but* a wild coincidence feels more and more outlandish.

"You'll just have to establish his last name next time you see him." Casey says matter-of-factly.

21

"*If* I ever see him again," I feel the need to clarify. I've never seen him before in all my four years of working there. It stands to reason I may never see him again. But it's a good plan to keep on the backburner, I suppose.

"I just have to ask," Suze starts. "You weren't, like, the only one who saw him, right?"

"Oh my God, no. Martha saw him too."

I made absolutely sure of it. Martha laughed at my question. *"How could I not see him? That boy was hand-SOM."*

"Okay, okay, sorry. I just wanted to make sure we weren't suddenly rooming with a schitzo."

I roll my eyes.

Even though the conversation leaves me feeling slightly more grounded in reality, I still spend all of my evening as well as half the night pouring through everything I have ever written about Ben. Not just from the story itself, which I spend a good chunk of time scrolling through for every detail about him, but also the notes app on my phone, a tattered spiraled notebook on my little desk, even some post-its I find in a dresser drawer—all the places I've ever scribbled ideas for my story or my characters.

There is *plenty* about Ben. Where he works, his hobbies, his unexpected sense of humor. I refresh my brain on all of it. If I ever see Real Ben again, I can quell my suspicions. My crazy, impossible suspicions.

Opening a blank Word document, I start typing out a file like I'm some private investigator and Ben is one of my prime suspects. *Ooh, maybe I can work with that—no, Jane, stay on track.*

Name: Benjamin "Ben" King
Age: 25
Occupation: Managing Editor for King Publishing
Hobbies: Reading, exercise, eating well, perusing shelves at used bookstores
Love Interest: Isabel "Izzie" Archer
Other Traits: Judgmental, unexpectedly gentle, observant, heart of gold

It feels good, my fingers flying over my keyboard with purpose. It's been so long. It feels so good, in fact, that I decide to compose a second list, one for Izzie, too:

Name: Isabel "Izzie" Archer (Named after the independent heroine of Henry James' expansive novel)
Age: 24
Occupation: Freelance Photographer
Hobbies: Creative photography, eating junk food, searching for purpose, only likes used bookstores for the aesthetic

Love Interest: Benjamin "Ben" King

Additional Traits: Independent, tries not to take life too seriously, secretly deep thinker, secretly lonely

By the time I'm finished with my lists, I feel as though I've caught up with old friends, my original purpose completely forgotten.

Name: Jane Campbell

Age: 22

Occupation: Barista. Sometimes moonlights as a proofreader

Hobbies: Hanging out with roommates, writing (ha), reading, eating junk food, conspiracy theories involving her own life (apparently)

Love Interest: Do near misses count?

Additional Traits: Social (translation: dependent on others), aimless

Really Jane? Is that all you can come up with? You're the main character of your own life, for goodness' sake.

I slam my laptop shut. Now I'm in a funk. And I lost track of my purpose. And my shift starts in five hours.

And I never made my soup!

THREE

When I considered the possibility of seeing Ben again last night with the roomies, it didn't occur to me that it might happen the very next day.

Sleep-deprived from my night of what now feels akin to stalking now that the man himself (or one eerily similar) is standing before me, my body goes very still at the sight of him. It's not even eight in the morning, and though strong black coffee is coursing through my veins, my extremities still lag several beats behind my brain. Or maybe it's my brain lagging behind my extremities. Hard to say.

Either way, I am not prepared for this. There's something about seeing him right now that makes me feel like I'm still sleeping.

"Jane," he says upon approaching the counter, and I jolt a little.

"How—"

"I'll share my methods when you share yours."

I purse my lips.

"That's what I thought."

He orders another Americano and pays with cash, so I can't even learn his last name from his receipt. It could be all in my head, but it almost seems intentional. He's watching me carefully.

Then again, my mind could just be playing yet another trick on me.

Now that the shock value has passed (well, most of it), I have a chance to get a good look at him in between making his drink. Martha's right: the guy is *hand-SOM*. And tall. My goodness, is he tall.

I wrote Ben to be a perfect 6'2 (because 6'1, Danny's height, didn't seem tall enough—all based on purely selfish reasons, myself clocking in at around 5'7), and if I had to guess, I'd say the man standing in front of me is exactly that.

His presence is certainly difficult to ignore—especially evident based on the furtive glances coming from the other patrons, mostly of the female variety. *See, not a schitzo.*

Ben catches me looking, and my cheeks grow warm. I tell myself it's the espresso steam.

When I set his drink down on the counter without incident, I'm so pleased I nearly pat myself on the back. But I'm already weird enough in his eyes; no need to go about making matters worse.

"Thank you," he says politely, if not a little on the dry side. It wouldn't faze me except that my research last night reminded me of his initial coolness.

"You're welcome," I level back in kind, for reasons unknown.

He takes his Americano and leaves. That's it. No confirmation, nothing.

I have to get that last name, even if it's the last thing I do.

Game on, Benjamin.

Looking down at my laptop, it's become painfully obvious that I'm now a full-fledged mental case.

I typed out my entire encounter with Ben, stretching it to two full pages, including my very real thoughts and feelings. What compelled me to do such a thing, I have no idea.

This, I keep to myself. No need to make Casey and Suze worry about my sanity; I'm certainly doing enough of that for all three of us.

27

I try to reason with myself that all art is based off of real life in some way, including written form, and I'm just pulling from my own real-life experiences for inspiration. But this is a going-nowhere scene. I even opened a fresh document to write it.

I shake my head slowly, chastising myself. Still, I hit CTRL-S.

Next order of business: isolate identifying features about Ben King I can use to establish Americano Ben's true identity.

All I need now is a bulletin board and some red yarn, and then I'd be 100% certifiable.

This time, when Ben comes back in next Friday around noon, I'm ready.

Benjamin King has a scar on his left shoulder from a childhood accident involving a brother I've yet to introduce. If Ben has that scar, we're golden.

Of course, solving one mystery opens the door to another, much bigger mystery—how in the heck does a fictional character come to life?—but I don't let myself think about that now. What am I supposed to do? See the walking, talking doppelganger of MY Benjamin King and just shrug my shoulders? Say, "*Eh, I'll let it be.*"? No!

A major problem to my evil plan presents itself almost immediately. Ben is wearing a crisp, buttoned up, white collared shirt. Of course.

I groan inwardly. Why does he have to be so uptight?

"Jane," he nods.

"You know that's not actually a greeting." I'm glad Martha's not here to see how I'm treating a customer. Truthfully, I don't know what's taking over me.

"Good afternoon, Jane."

"Better. Good afternoon, Ben."

As I make his Americano, I devise a Plan B. I'll just have to figure something else out. I have a whole list of identifying features at home, not to mention in my brain. Or I can wait for him to wear a t-shirt. I mean, it's not like I can just spill coffee on him to get him to take off his shirt...

I smile to myself, shaking my head slowly. Right, it's not like I can do *that*. It would be too cruel. It's a nice shirt, and it would probably inconvenience him for the rest of the day.

Right. It's not like I can do *that*.

And yet, no sooner do the words "you're all set" come out of my mouth does my foot happen to catch on the squishy floor mat. I lurch forward, towards Ben, lidless cup in hand, and with one surreptitious flick of the wrist, Ben's chest is doused in Americano.

It's quite a sight to behold, and the shock on my face is very real.

"Oh my God, I am so sorry. Oh my God."

Ben grits his teeth. "It's fine."

"No, it's not. Let me, uh—" I'm floundering. I was kind of hoping the heat of the liquid would cause him to immediately remove his shirt, but instead he just angles forward so the fabric doesn't stick to his body. He's also staring at me, eyes intense. Oh God, he hates me.

I quickly grab a stack of napkins and rush back to him, wiping furiously at his chest.

He sighs. "You really don't have to—"

I gasp dramatically. "Oh my God, it's totally soaked through. Here, let me just—" I get to work on his top button, fully aware of how scandalous it looks for me to be undressing a man in the middle of my place of work, but I can't jump ship now. I'm past the point of no return, baby.

"Uhh..." is all Ben manages to say, and I don't blame him. I'd be at a loss for words, too.

Three buttons down. The white t-shirt underneath is visible. It's now or never.

I swiftly reach up and yank the left side of his shirt down just a smidge, revealing the skin beneath.

"Jane?" someone half-laughs behind us.

I let go of Ben and spin around to see Danny gaping at us.

"What the heck is going on here?" His eyebrows are practically touching the ceiling.

"I spilled." I gesture lamely behind me. "You probably want another Americano," I say to Ben, turning as I do, but I stop short when I see his expression. His head is tilted to one side, and he's looking at me like I'm a creature in a zoo.

I return to the safety of the espresso machine. "Did I mention how sorry I am?" I ask him meekly. Still staring. "You're kinda scary, you know that?"

Before I give him his new drink (again), I ring up a gift card as an apology. Mostly because I feel bad, but also to ensure he comes back.

Because while this Ben doesn't have a scar, he *does* have a tiny tattoo of a crown.

Almost as if his last name could be royal.

"You *spilled?* All over his *chest?*" Danny asks incredulously after Ben leaves without a word. He didn't even thank me for the gift card, but I suppose I deserve that.

"Yes. Is that so hard to believe?"

"It is, actually. You never spill. In the entire time I've worked here, you've never so much as splashed water onto the floor."

31

This much is true. I even keep a hand towel tucked into my apron to wipe up any minor spills. Stupid Danny and his observational prowess.

"First time for everything, I guess. What do you want?"

"Sheesh. Large latte and a nicer attitude, please and thank you."

"Sorry," I sigh, taking his payment and getting to work on his drink. "I have a lot on my mind."

Like, if Ben has a crown tattoo then could his last name be King? And if his last name is King then why doesn't he have the scar? Why would he have a tattoo I never wrote?

"No worries. Hey, did you see the shop next door is closing again?"

"Yeah," I laugh. "I wonder how long it'll last this time."

The antiques shop next door, cleverly named ANTIQUES, has been "closing" for years. Every once in a while, the owner, Eve, puts out a sign for a closing sale, usually a "50%-off-everything-must-go" kind of deal, and then just... never closes.

At first it brought as much of a rush as my over-easy eggs. I would drive to work in anticipation, thinking, *Will today be the day ANTIQUES finally closes—for good?*

It never did. The drama soon lost its appeal, and now when I see the big closing sign out front, I roll my eyes.

"Wanna make a bet?" His eyes are full of mischief.

"No way, you totally ripped me off last time."

"I did not! It's not my fault you're a terrible gambler."

I snort. "Yeah, okay, Danny P."

It takes longer to write today's scene in the new document not-so-cleverly titled "Americano." I even include the part when Danny steps in and our conversation about ANTIQUES, just for fun.

Then I join the roomies in the living room to rehash what I've done.

"You *what?*" Suze asks while Casey chokes on her kombucha.

"I took it too far, right?"

"Well as long as you're *aware*," Casey guffaws.

"I had to do it! Don't you want to know what I saw?"

This catches their attention. "You mean…" Suze starts. "He has the scar?" Casey finishes.

I take a deep breath and square my shoulders for dramatic effect. "No."

Both girls deflate. "Jane," Casey says tiredly while Suze rubs her temple.

"Buuuut, he *did* have a tattoo of a crown."

They perk up again. "Seems like something a King would have, no?"

"Wait," Suze asks, looking confused. "Does Ben King have a crown tattoo?"

"That's the strange part. No, he does not. I never wrote about any tattoo."

"Weird," Casey says. "But you did write about the scar?"

"Of course…" My voice trails off. Did I?

I rush into my room, grab my laptop, and rush back out. In my story, I do a quick CTRL-F and type in the word "scar." *No matches.* "Huh."

"'Huh'? Does that mean you didn't write about a scar?"

"I guess not. I just planned on writing it in at some point." I pictured the scene long ago: Izzie noticing the scar for the first time, brushing her fingertips across it; Ben sharing the story behind it, the most relaxed she's ever seen him. I must have imagined it so vividly that I thought I already wrote it. But no, their relationship hasn't reached that point yet.

"Interesting…" Suze says.

I look at my roommates over my laptop's screen. "You know what I need? A second opinion. And a third."

They both groan.

"Come on, you already work from home! Just bring your stuff to the coffee shop on Monday and observe Ben when he comes in."

"*If* he comes in, after what you did to him today," Casey points out.

"That, my dear friend, is why I gave him a gift card for his troubles."

"Genius." Suze looks impressed. "I'm in. I'm curious, anyway."

We both look expectantly at Casey, who doesn't take long to relent. "Fine. We'll see if he's as good-looking as you say he is."

"Excellent. Now all you need to do is read this." I open the page from the other night when I listed all of Ben King's physical features, mannerisms, even some quotes from the book to establish the way he speaks and email them both a copy for reference. It's only a couple pages long, but by their reactions you'd think I've just handed them a Tolstoy novel.

Still, they read. I bum around on my phone as they do so, trying to ignore the twist in my stomach I inevitably feel any time I let someone read something I wrote.

Casey and Suze have only ever read carefully selected excerpts from my story since I'm admittedly too chicken to share the whole thing. To be perfectly honest, I don't know what scares me more: outright criticism or false praise.

Once they're all caught up, I flash them an expectant look. "So, Monday?"

"Monday," they reply in unison.

35

FOUR

Spring, as it would seem, is back on in Minnesota.

What little snow we got last week has completely disappeared, just in time for a new week. You don't just feel it in the air, you sense it in the people, too. Today, everyone has a skip in their step, everyone shares a smile (and a little extra tip). The relief is palpable. Soon, May will be here with its blooms; for now, the sun alone will suffice.

Casey and Suze share a table along the far wall, right across from the counter, the perfect viewing location. They've been here since seven in the morning, just to make sure they don't miss a Ben sighting. Every time the door opens they both look up from their laptops. If it's a man, they then look to me. If I shake my head, they go back to work.

This goes on for hours. The girls are getting antsy. I can tell, because I'm the antsiest of us all.

Just when I think he won't show, that he was too offended by my antics after all, in he comes just before the end of my shift. The girls look to me, read my expression, and go back to staring openly at Ben, wide-eyed.

Casey gapes at him, then looks down at her laptop, where my list presumably sits open on her screen, then back up to Ben, dumbfounded. Suze just stares. I feel like an old pro compared to the two of them.

"How's the shirt?" I ask timidly in lieu of a greeting.

"DOA."

I wince. "Did I mention that I'm sorry?"

"Several times. Don't worry about it, it lived a good long life."

I blink in surprise. Gracious and good humored—now that I know I didn't write. It's certainly not unwelcome, however.

I glance behind him to see the girls hanging on our every word. Good. I'm going to ask about the tattoo. It's less invasive than what I did to him yesterday, anyway.

Before I can get the words out, he's saying something else. It's so unexpected I have to ask him to repeat himself. "I said if you really wanted to make it up to me, I have something in mind."

"What? Oh! The shirt." Why am I so slow? "Yes, absolutely. Anything I can do."

"When does your shift end?"

I look up at the wall clock. "Two minutes ago."

Ben actually smiles. Granted, it's a lopsided, plotting kind of smile, but a smile, nonetheless. *What the heck is going on?*

"Excellent. There's a ramen place down the street. You're buying."

My mouth drops into a little "o." In my peripheral, I can see that Casey and Suze's have as well.

"Uhh…" I flick my eyes imperceptibly behind his shoulder to where Casey and Suze are beckoning me forwards with their hands and mouthing the word, "GO!"

Ben's forehead crinkles and he starts to turn around (okay, not as good at subtlety as I thought) but I quickly stop him by agreeing to his request. "Sure, why not? Lead the way!"

I clock out quickly and shoot my coworker in the backroom a quick farewell before gathering up my jacket and bag and meeting Ben by the door.

I can feel the energy at the girls' table as I pass by, and they watch me with stars in their eyes. I suppose novel confusion aside, I *am* leaving with a very handsome, very tall man. Still, I can't wait to hear their conclusions later.

It's only when we've started walking down the street that I realize he never got his Americano—never even asked for it. Was his entire reason for showing up at all today to get a form of repayment for his ruined shirt? And am I ridiculous for hoping it's something more than that?

As we pass ANTIQUES, I read the big white posters on the front window:

CLOSING SALE. EVERYTHING MUST GO. 50-70% OFF.

"That's new," I mutter to myself. Normally it's more of a 30-50 range.

"What?"

"Oh, just the antiques place. This isn't the first closing sale, but I've never seen such high markdowns."

"Funny. Maybe it's closing for real this time."

Oddly, the thought makes me rather sad. "Nah," I wave the thought away. "That place will outlive us all."

Ben laughs through his teeth, like "tsh."

The rest of the walk, I tell him about the other times ANTIQUES has advertised major closing sales, the bets I've lost to coworkers (ahem, Danny P.), and the owner, Eve, a Hmong woman who makes the word "petite" seem inadequate. I'm babbling. I know it, he knows it, yet I can't stop.

"No seriously, she'd probably come up right about…" I flatten my hand and slice it towards Ben's hipbone… "*Here.*"

He laughs more heartily at this. Then we reach the ramen place. It's a mid-tier ramen joint, one I frequent simply because of its convenient location, whereas my favorite place is more downtown. Top-tier, expensive, fusion-y. Only for the most special of occasions. I don't voice these thoughts as we approach the counter, however.

Ben orders the tonkotsu and a side of kimchi; I stick with my usual shio base and an order of dumplings to share.

Once nestled at a small table by the corner, silence kicks in. I gear myself up for another round of nervous babble when Ben finally speaks.

"Thank you," is what he says.

"It's the least I could do after what happened last week. Though… you know you're a very forward person, right?" I hope that's the least-offensive way to let him know it's usually considered strange for men to ask women to comp their lunch out of the blue.

"I do know that, it drives my coworkers nuts."

Ding. A lightbulb goes off in my brain. Here's Ben, right in front of me, and all there is to do while we wait for our food is talk. Or in other words, *investigate.*

"Oh yeah?" I ask, clenching my fists in my lap to stop them from shaking in anticipation. "What do you do?" I sound like my windpipe is blocked. Very smooth.

"I work at a publishing company"—EEK—"as a Managing Editor."

Okay, Jane, no reason to freak out. That's only exactly what my fictional Ben King does for a living. It could still be a coincidence. Crazier things have happened, right?

"Oh?" I squeak, struggling for something else to say when my thoughts are so loud. "You must… like… books… then?"

Despite the question, I know he does. In fact, he and Izzie meet in a bookstore.

Stop it. Ben King and Izzie meet in a bookstore. The person sitting across from you isn't—can't be—couldn't possibly—

My thoughts are interrupted by a server setting tall bowls of ramen in front of us. I dumbly gesture for Ben to try one of the dumplings, then pick up a piece of kimchi with my chopsticks without asking. Ben doesn't seem to mind, in any case. The kimchi is good. Really good. I wonder why I've never tried it before.

A sip of my ramen broth soothes me in more ways than one. I have time to think as I slurp the noodles, munch on a dumpling, sip some water, and repeat. And what I think is this:

41

It doesn't matter whether the person slurping noodles in front of me is character out of a book or the freaking crown prince of Prussia. All I know is he's very real. Shouldn't that be enough?

I decide to stop asking questions, except for the ones that come up naturally in conversation. The more I relax, the more I begin to enjoy myself.

Ben, too, seems to be having a good time. He laughs more at my jokes and seems genuinely interested when I talk about my life. I tell him about my roommates (leaving out their earlier presence, of course), about Common Ground and my favorite and least favorite parts of the job.

He tells me about his life, too, and I try my very best not to filter any of it through the King Lens. It works, for the most part, and I enjoy hearing about the weirdest books he's ever had to read as a Managing Editor, and some of the more well-known titles he was privileged to work on.

I do not ask him the name of this publishing company.

In my book, it's owned by Ben's family. King Publishing. But that is something that he waits to reveal to Izzie until after she's already fallen for him. Not because he thinks she's materialistic and he wants to be loved for who he is (because that would be too cliché), but because he's somewhat embarrassed by his wealthy, quirky family.

No, I do not ask the name of the company, nor do I ask about his family. And you know what? I have a wonderful time.

We part ways back at the coffee shop, where our cars are parked. But before we do, Ben stops at the corner and turns to face me. "This was fun. We should do it again."

I blink hard. "Yeah, it was. We should."

He raises his eyebrows.

"I swear I'm not always this agreeable."

He laughs. "Later, Jane."

"Later, Ben."

He goes down one corner; I, down another.

Casey and Suze still have stars in their eyes when I arrive back at the apartment, but they have to forgo asking any questions for the time being as the workday is still in full swing.

"Later, we should go out to eat so we can talk!" Suze suggests excitedly.

"She *just* went out to eat," Casey calls from her bedroom/office.

"Oh, right. Drinks, then?"

I shoot her with a finger gun and click my teeth, the universal sign for *heck yeah.*

It'll be nice to have a few hours alone, anyway. Once settled in bed, I plug my laptop in and boot it up.

Just because I've decided to take it easy on my conspiracy theories doesn't mean I can't still use the inspiration. "Americano" is already open on the screen when it finally comes to life, and I scroll to the next blank page to write as much as I remember from today, as I remember it. The scenes, the senses, the dialogue. Casey and Suze make an appearance in this one, at the beginning.

Every scene in this document exists separate from each other, running concurrently in timeline only. Maybe someday I'll do a little CTRL-style copy and pasting to make it all sound a little less crazy. For now, I tell myself it's a literary form of journaling.

Once I've felt I included everything, I go back through and restructure sentences not just from today's entry but also the past few as well, maybe tweak a little dialogue. Old habits.

The entire process takes so long that by the time I'm done, Casey is poking her head in saying she wants to go out to eat after all, and, since the only food I have in the fridge are leftovers I'm less inclined to partake of, I easily agree.

We choose an easy spot for dinner: a modern taco place within walking distance that also happens to serve tasty margaritas. Win, win.

The hostess barely sets the waters down before the gabbing kicks into high gear, interrupted only by the waiter taking our orders and asking if we want chips and salsa (answer: always.).

"Okay, I can see why you were freaking out. He really does look like the physical embodiment of your character," Casey says. "And he really has the same first name?"

"And you still don't know what his last name is?" Suze adds before I can say anything.

"Yes," I say to Casey, "and no," I say to Suze. "There's something else too... He does the same thing for a living."

They gasp. "Managing editor?" Suze asks. See, I knew my lists would be helpful.

"*Yes*. He told me today."

"Okay, wow. *Wow*."

"Yup."

We all stare at the table for minute, simultaneously processing. The margaritas arrive just in time.

Casey takes two long dredges from hers before speaking again. "Okay, but like how did it go today? Walk us through it."

"Yeah, what was he like? How were you together? Don't leave anything out."

I give them exactly what they asked for: a fully detailed version of today's events, including my own personal commentary, thoughts, opinions, as well as some validating questions, such as, "*What do you think that means?*", "*Do you think he thinks I'm pretty?*"

I start from the moment we left the coffee shop, from my nervous chatting, to what we ordered. I relay what we talked about, how I decided to stop thinking about my story so I could be more in the moment. Finally, I tell them how Ben said we should do it again. That last part causes them both to squeal.

"Okay, hear me out for a second," Suze says cautiously. "But what if—"

I cut her off. "I can't think like that. I mean, I've tried. It's been driving me nuts. I keep asking myself what I would do if he somehow *was*... But I just don't know. It's easier to just see what happens, right?"

"Yeah," Casey says, albeit a little weakly. Suze says nothing.

"What, you think I should keep spilling hot coffee on him until I figure out who he is and where he comes from?"

They roll their eyes. "Well *no*, of course not. You just have to think long-term."

There it is. *Long-term.* I hate those stupid little words, making me feel like my future is waiting and one misstep today will mess the whole thing up.

46

"I can't believe I'm saying this, because it means we're as crazy as you are," Suze leans across the table, "but how sustainable would an author/character relationship be?"

"Author/*authee*?" Casey mutters to herself. Then she giggles. My eyes flick to her half-empty margarita glass. Girl's a lightweight.

"I mean," Suze continues thoughtfully, "isn't that as bad as a teacher/student relationship?" She sees my grimace. "No, no, hear me out. Like, one party knows more than the other. One party knows better. One has more of the facts." Each time she says something, she gestures like she's chopping an invisible carrot in the palm of her hand. Suze rarely means business, but when she does, you listen up.

"But, but, but..." Struggling to come up with a decent counterargument, I resort to pouting. "Ben's an adult! He's older than me, even!"

Correction: Ben *King* is older than me. The Ben I ate ramen with today could be anything, anyone. It's more difficult to separate fact from fiction than I thought it would be.

Suze has a point, though. It would be unfair, should this insane theory actually come to fruition, to know more about someone than I'm letting on. Much, much more. Instagram stalking is one thing. Me? I'm on a whole other playing field.

"Oh, whatever." Casey waves her hand dismissively. "He's hot!" The words, while true, come out just a little too loud, and other patrons glance over at us.

"And on that note," Suze says, signaling for the check.

We stroll leisurely back to our apartment, chattering away about the things we can't wait to do when it gets warmer, like bike around the lakes, go up north to Suze's family's cabin (which we get free rein over at least once every summer), achieve an even tan.

By the time we reach the apartment, Casey's walked off what little buzz she had, which is all as well, since it's a Monday night and she has to work in the morning.

We take turns getting ready for bed in our one tiny bathroom, then we're exchanging goodnights and flipping off all the lights.

Laying in the dark, waiting for sleep, I think of Ben.

Which Ben, I honestly can't say.

FIVE

It's raining Thursday morning as I drive to work so early in the morning that it's still dark out. Opening shifts start at 5:30 AM, and like most mornings, I have to remind myself every two seconds that soon I'll have access to as much freshly-brewed coffee as I want.

Listening to the raindrops pelt my windshield, I can't help but think that it would've been a good writing day. It also reminds me of the day I accepted a job at Common Ground, nearly four years ago.

When I took the job two months after high school graduation, I was naïve enough to believe it was a temporary fix, something to pay what little bills I had and then I would move on to something decidedly better. I would look back on my time as a barista fondly, and graciously stop in for a latte on my way to my Dream Job™.

The only problem was that Dream Job™ was nothing more than a vague notion that changed all the time. For a while, the longest while, it was to write a novel. Whether or not it had any publishing potential simply didn't matter—it was something I enjoyed and provided a sense of purpose previously unknown to me, and if I'm being honest, unknown to me since.

So at Common Ground I remained—my only employment, save for a freelance copyediting gig for a prolific mommy blogger who can't edit to save her life, but who does pay generously per article.

The money garnered from copyediting supplemented my income enough that I was able to move out of my parents' suburban home. Of course, I would never have been able to afford living in South Minneapolis if it weren't for Casey and Suze and the unused dining room of their two-bedroom apartment, something they were happy to give up in exchange for the lower rent.

My parents are happy for me. They've never once made me feel less-than for not pursuing the same course as my peers; the "safe" course. School, career, etc. All these years, I've had nothing but support as I attempted (unsuccessfully) to figure things out.

"If you're happy, we're happy," they say, a loving monster with two heads.

I should feel relieved, but I don't. Sometimes I wish they were more disappointed in me. At least then I'd actually have a reason to avoid their calls.

No one knows this, not even Casey and Suze.

I don't like thinking about the future.

And I definitely don't like thinking about what I'm good at. It's a short and questionable list.

I mean, there has to be something wrong with your life when the most exciting part of your day is making an egg, right?

It rains all morning, varying only in intensity.

Rain affects business in different ways. Sometimes, it means the coffee shop will be dead all day, save for a customer or two who park themselves at a table for hours on end. Other times, we're even busier than a normal, non-rainy day.

Today it's the latter. I'm grateful for it, since staying busy is the only thing that helps me forget how tired I am, even with three cups of coffee making their way through my system.

Near the end of my shift, Danny strolls in chattier than ever, so after making his avocado toast and clocking out, I sit opposite him and rest my head on the table while he chatters on about his day. He doesn't seem to mind my lack of participation in the conversation.

"Some May Day, huh?" he grumbles, looking forlornly out the window.

I laugh, even though he wasn't making a joke. I hadn't even realized today marks a new month.

"Well, I should go. See you on the flippity-flop."

Once he leaves, there's nothing holding me back from doing the same, except that it's raining harder now and my seat is warm.

My phone buzzes and it takes an embarrassing amount of effort to pull it out of my bag. It's a text from my mom. *Cleaning out basement this weekend, come help or we'll throw all your toys away.*

Psh. Like that's a threat. I'm twenty-two years old, for heavens' sake.

I leave the text alone for now. Spending my weekend in a basement isn't my idea of fun, though I know I'll end up there anyway. Not for the toys, or the countless stuffed animals, but for the artifacts of my past that deserve to be preserved, or at the very least, looked at one last time.

That last thought makes me sad. I shake it off, instead gathering up my bag and umbrella and heading towards the door.

Outside, the moment I've extended my umbrella, Eve from ANTIQUES materializes in front of me. "Can you help?" she asks in a thick accent.

It's a vague request, but English is not her first language. I nod and she gestures for me to follow.

I can count the times I've actually been inside ANTQUES on one hand. My life doesn't exactly have a high demand for old stuff, and you can only peruse the same rows of shelves so many times before you start to memorize the contents.

While the shelves are slightly barer (the "closing" sale must be going well), the interior is otherwise the same.

I follow Eve over to the front counter, where she has a new, bigger poster. This one reads: CLOSING SOON. EVERYTHING MUST GO. 70-80% OFF.

Sheesh. How does Eve expect to make any money with these markdowns? Maybe she's trying to make room for new stock. Who knows?

She points firmly to the poster, then the front window, where the only empty space left is on the upper right-hand corner, way too high for Eve to reach. I feel like a giant standing next to her—a big, monstrous American.

Suze once told me we're bigger than people from other countries because of all the hormones in our food. Now, standing next to a very petite Asian woman, I wonder if that's true.

Eve looks at me expectantly to make sure I understand. I nod, and she hands me a roll of duct tape.

Before I stick the sign on the window, I look down at Eve to make sure it's going exactly where she wants it. She nods approvingly, and I press the tape into the window.

It amazes me how universal nodding is. You can have a whole conversation with nothing but gestures.

"Tall!" she laughs, and so do I. "Thank you!"

"No problem! See you."

I leave Eve to her business.

At home, I watch TV until it's acceptably late enough to make dinner, and then I watch more TV until turning in hours earlier than the girls, as I have yet another opening shift in the morning.

I don't complain about the early mornings to Casey and Suze anymore. Not since Casey once said, "Get a normal job that starts at nine, then!" in such a dismissive tone that I've never been able to forget it.

Normal job. As if Common Ground isn't a normal job. I have a set schedule, I get a paycheck every two weeks. Isn't that *normal?*

Of course, I know what Casey meant. Barista-ing tends to be a rather transitory job, something I've personally witnessed firsthand over the years as people come and go. In the minds of many people, my roommates included, it's a job for high schoolers and college students. Something you do for a little extra spending money until you graduate and get a "real job."

Normal job. Real job. The words that haunt me the most.

Truthfully, I'm comfortable where I am. Plus, Martha and I have a good relationship. That is to say, I know the shop backwards and forwards and never make mistakes. She's made it very clear that she appreciates the stability I provide, and I like feeling needed. Appreciated.

Still, I'd be lying if I said I never fantasized about a 9-5. My sleep schedule would be so consistent. I'd be so well-rested.

Nah, I always remind myself when the thought pops up. *Consistency is overrated.*

Much to my delight, and the delight of every single one of my customers, yesterday's rain paved the way for a rather sunny Friday.

There's nothing Minnesotans love talking about more than the weather.

"What's that big yellow thing in the sky?" I ask a few different regulars while they wait for their beverages. This one always gets a laugh. It's one of the many anecdotes I like to keep in my back pocket.

Around nine, just when the first rush begins to die down, Danny P. walks in, then a middle-aged woman, then Ben.

This should be interesting.

Danny orders seamlessly enough, until he exclaims, "What's that big yellow thing in the sky!" in a voice I can only assume is a botched imitation of my own.

"Hey!" I say defensively. We worked together too long. He lets out an evil little laugh and moves down to catch up with Martha at the espresso machine.

Next, the middle-aged woman flashes a friendly smile and looks me directly in the eye as she asks very politely for a skim latte. My favorite kind of customer. I hold her eye contact and return the smile.

"You have lovely eyes," the woman says kindly as she hands over her credit card.

"Oh! Um, thank you," I blush. I wouldn't normally be so flustered except that Ben is overhearing all of it.

"I just *have* to ask…"

Lord, here we go. The question that always follows compliments. An inevitability, at this point. *What are you?*

"What is your last name?"

Different question, same ask.

"Campbell," I reply, not at all surprised when her face registers confusion.

This is what happens when you have a very white surname and a very Arab face.

Even though I'm never obligated to elaborate further, I explain: "My mom is Palestinian."

"Ahh!" she says, delighted. "How unique!"

"Halfsies!" Danny suddenly interjects, extending his hand for a high-five—which I swiftly accept in the name of Solidarity. The woman witnesses this with an even wider smile on her face, and Danny visibly glows at the opportunity to entertain.

I give her the receipt and she moves down the counter, seamlessly transitioning into a conversation with Martha and Danny at the espresso machine.

Finally, it's Ben's turn.

"Hey! Americano?"

He nods, and I ring him up.

"Palestinian, huh?"

I glance up to see that his eyes are scanning my face, searching for the evidence. Almond eyes: Check. Olive skin: Check. Arab nose: Check. Check. Check. I take after my mother so much, you'd never even guess that half of all my DNA is white.

"That's fun," he says.

I snort. "Super fun."

"So listen," he says. "Would you want to hang out later? I have the afternoon off."

His question takes me by surprise. But of course I say yes. How could I not?

"Great. Meet here at the end of your shift? Same time as Monday?"

I nod. I already can't wait to tell Casey and Suze, and nothing's even happened yet.

After they've all left, Martha sidles up to me as I'm refilling my mug of coffee and asks in a low voice, "Did I just overhear that fine specimen asking you out?"

As flattered as I am that she thinks it was a straight up asking-out, I tell her we're just hanging out. "We actually went to the ramen place down the street on Monday. Kind of a spontaneous thing since I owed him for ruining his shirt."

She looks confused. "'Ruining his shirt'? Fill me in."

"Oh, right." I look at her meekly. "I kinda spilled coffee all over his chest last week."

"What? But you never spill!"

I laugh. "That's exactly what Danny P. said."

"Mmm. Poor Danny P.," she says wistfully.

I look sideways at her. "Huh?"

She takes a deep breath and sighs as she speaks. "It just must be hard for him to see another man making moves on you, is all."

I nearly spit out my coffee. "What?" I choke.

She gives me a pitiful look, like I can't be helped. "Oh, never mind."

But I can't just *never mind.* "Danny and I are just friends! He doesn't think about me like that."

More pity. "It's true!" I exclaim emphatically.

"Okay, okay! I'm just teasing!" She raises her hands defensively, and I finally start to relax. "But I still think you two would make adorable babies."

"Martha!"

This gets her laughing. It takes me a few more minutes to see the humor in what she was saying.

There's no way Danny P. would be jealous of Ben. He doesn't like me enough. If he did, he would've asked me out years ago, and he never did.

I shake the thought away, replacing it with a new one: I'm hanging out with Ben again. In a few short hours. And Martha thought it was a date!

I can't help it. In the backroom, I pull out my phone and open the "Roomies" group chat. *Guess who just asked to meet me at the end of my shift TODAY?*

Casey is the first to reply. *Benny Boy???*

Ding ding ding!! And please don't call him that lol.

Ugh, fine. What are you going to do??

IDK!! Who cares!

OMG, is all Suze contributes.

"Could you make an avocado toast to go?" Martha calls from the front.

"Sure!" I slide my phone away and get back to work.

Just as he said, Ben returns at noon on the dot.

I wave goodbye to Martha, trying not to blush at the positively scandalous expression on her face as I leave, and pick up the iced latte I made for myself.

It's incredibly nice out. Every component of spring is at play today, except for the leaves. One of these days, we'll all just wake up to green trees. It's Mother Nature's way.

Ben lays out his plan as we walk to his car. "So I was thinking we'd do lunch first—anything you're particularly hungry for?—and then just walk around, see what happens?"

It's exactly the kind of plan I like best. Go with the flow, involves food. I'm especially intrigued by the *"see what happens"* part.

"Hmm…" I think for a moment. "I'm in the mood for a sandwich."

"A sandwich," he repeats slowly.

"A good one."

"Okay. That can be arranged."

We climb into his car, a sleek black sedan with a classy leather interior. Something, I can't help but think, a man with a rich family might own.

It's a short drive to the destination: a small French café right off one of the major lakes. I've passed it many times without ever really thinking about it. I never would've guessed it could be a lunch-y, sandwich-y kind of place.

"You wanted a good sandwich? This place has the best *croque monsieures*."

"What's a *croque monsieur*?"

"Oh, you'll see."

As it turns out, a *croque monsieur* is basically a fancy way of saying *ham sandwich*. But I'll be darned if it isn't the best ham sandwich I've ever had in my life.

"Holy crap," I say with a mouthful after my first bite. "*Holy crap.*"

"Yup," Ben says, also with a mouthful of toasted bread, ham, and gruyere cheese.

I take another large bite, pointing furiously at the slice in my hand before I can speak again. "This is a game-changing sandwich. I can feel it."

This makes Ben laugh.

All conversation is put on hold until we're finished eating.

We just sit there for a while, digesting, until Ben suggests we walk it off.

"I don't want to walk it off. I want it to make a home in my stomach forever."

He shakes his head, eyes gleaming with amusement. "We can come back."

At this, I perk up. "Then yes, let's walk it off."

Ben picks up the bill, holds the door open for me, and then we're standing on a street corner, wondering which way to go.

The left looks less busy, so we go left. We stroll leisurely up and down Hennepin Avenue, talking, people-watching. It's… nice. Really nice.

I learn a little more about Ben. He works downtown but lives closer to the neighborhood where Common Ground is, thus his frequent visits. Apparently, he had no idea we existed until a couple weeks ago when his normal commute detoured to our street. The next day, the day I said his name aloud, was his first visit.

We turn onto a quieter street and pass an old bookstore, which Ben stops in front of. "Can we go in? I need a new book."

What a book dork. I smile and follow him in.

It's a new and used bookstore I've been to only once before, one with high wooden shelves and a musty smell. The store is much deeper than it looks from the outside, stretching so far I can't see the back wall.

Ben turns down the aisle of new releases while I pick up the first book I see on the table by the door. I flip it over to read the blurb on the back. Set it back down. Then I give up and just follow Ben.

Watching Ben pull books down from high shelves, looking for his next pile of reads, another scene flashes in my mind.

One of Ben and Izzie on the day they meet.

Ben never rushed his browsing. It was almost a religious experience. Sacred. Every aisle was worth examining, a new denomination to be sampled. Classical fiction, mystery, historical, nonfiction, biographies, memoires—it was all paper gold. He never thought about how the spines would look on the extensive bookshelves all over his apartment.

Izzie, too, perused the aisles in a slow, calculated manner; but unlike Ben, she wasn't looking for something to read. Oh no, books, like everything else, was something to look at, something to photograph, but only if it was right, only if it had the exact aesthetic she was looking for.

There, up near a tall man's head, was the perfect hardcover. Red, eye-catching, vintage-looking. Izzie needed it immediately.

Ben saw the dainty hand first, reaching for a book he knew and loved. His eyes followed it down to the petite brunette smiling over the cover, and Ben, for the first time maybe ever, thought he might be smitten.

"You have good taste," he found himself saying, before she could walk away. "The author lived as a migrant worker for six years before he ever started writing it."

Izzie had not a single clue as to what this man was talking about. She glanced down at the book in her hand. "Oh! I'm not going to read it. I'm going to dismantle it for a photoshoot."

Ben was no longer smitten. He was absolutely flabbergasted.

To him, mutilating one piece of art for the sake of another is a disgrace, and he tells her as much. To Izzie, his logic doesn't make much sense. Something crackles between them. They think it's instant dislike, but I know better. It's attraction.

I feel like Izzie now, reaching for a book near Real Ben's head, and feel a little thrill when he asks if I've read it. But unlike Izzie, I have no disdain for the man beside me. None at all. He shares an interesting fact about the book in my hand.

I feel like I'm dreaming.

If this really is some crazy coincidence the universe has for some reason decided to throw at me, then so be it. It's a pretty good one.

I buy the book. I don't know if I'll ever read it, but Ben likes it so I have to have it. Casey and Suze will rightfully call me pathetic.

He returns me to Common Ground an hour later, but not before gesturing for me to hand over my phone, which I do, unlocked.

He types what I assume is his number, then his own phone buzzes in his other hand. "Last name: Campbell," he says more to himself as he enters in my information.

"Thanks for today. I think…" He pauses, and I suddenly feel the need to hold my breath. "I think this… we…" Still holding my breath.

Whatever it was, he seems to change his mind. I can almost see the flip switch across his face. "…should be friends."

I deflate a little. That can't be what he was going to say from the start of that sentence.

"I agree." What else can I do?

He smiles, I smile, then I climb out of his car and start walking towards my own.

When I finally glance down at my phone, I nearly drop it.

When Ben filled out his contact information, he included his last name. Like it's no big deal. Like he hasn't been sneaky about it this whole time. And now I know.

Really, I've known all along.

First name: Benjamin.

Last name: King.

SIX

I'm numb when I unlock the door to our apartment. Still numb when I sit on the closest chair. And numb yet when Casey and Suze emerge from their rooms to ask me how today went.

"It's him," I whisper.

"Huh?" They both move closer.

"It's... *him.*"

This time they hear me. "No way," Suze says. I dumbly hold out my phone with Ben's contact information right there on the screen, and they gasp. They wear matching expressions of surprise and horror. Clearly, they didn't think it was actually possible. Not like I did.

"I have to sit down," Casey announces to no one in particular before crashing on the couch. Suze stays glued to the floor.

"Jane, what are you thinking? Talk to us."

I open my mouth, but no words come out.

Suze takes action. She disappears into the kitchen and returns moments later with three short glasses of clear liquid. Judging by the smell, it ain't water. "Shoot it," she instructs Casey and me.

I'm not sure how helpful this can be, but it's a nice gesture, so I do as she says. So does Casey. She takes our glasses back to the kitchen and brings them back full.

Surprisingly (or maybe *unsurprisingly*) I do feel more inclined to talk after the second round.

"What am I supposed to do now?"

"What do you mean?" Suze asks.

"Just like you said, how can I be friends with him when I already know everything about him? When I... when I... *invented* him!" I wail. I feel like I'm going to be sick.

"That's not technically true," Casey points out. "You were wrong about the scar."

"How did this happen? Why? This is crazy, right? We're all crazy."

"Wait." Suze doesn't answer my question. "Did you say 'friends?'"

I laugh dryly. "Oh yeah, on top of everything else, he friendzoned me."

"I'm sure that's not true. I'm sure he was just nervous—wait. Do you think he knows who you are, too?"

"No way," I say firmly. "There's just no way."

"What if…" Casey theorizes, "…you met him years ago and thought he was attractive but forgot about him, and the name and description you used in your book is just like a weird Freudian slip-type thing?"

Suze and I stare at her.

"You know, like how the people we see in dreams are just strangers off the street."

I snap my fingers. "You could be on to something."

But then I remember if this theory were true, I most likely would've met him before he ever started working at the publishing company. I tell them as much. "Well, I tried," Casey says, leaning back into the couch cushion.

"Jane, you should keep seeing him," Suze suddenly says.

"But you're the one who said—"

"I know, but that was before we knew. Now, think about it. This is a gift. What author gets to actually talk to their character? This might be exactly what you need to finish the story!"

"Huh. I haven't thought about that…"

"She's right," Casey says. "Why question it? I say just roll with it."

This is a gift. Just roll with it.

68

"You really think so? I ask, looking between the two of them. This is no longer the time to sugar coat their answers. What they say next will determine what I decide.

"Yes," they answer resolutely and firmly.

And that's all I need.

They must see it in my face, because Casey smiles. "So," she starts, her voice mischievous. "When do we get to meet him?"

SEVEN

The first thing I notice when I pull into the driveway at my parents' house is that our cottonwood trees are starting to shed their sticky little buds.

When I step out of my car, I notice they already litter my tires. By the time I get to the front door, they're all over the bottom of my shoe, too.

I let myself in. "Helloooo," I call out softly, so I don't scare them. That was an adjustment when I first moved out: coming home to visit or do laundry (usually both) and nearly giving my parents a heart attack when they come downstairs to find me digging in the fridge or lounging on the living room sofa.

No answer. I hear faint noises coming from the basement and follow the sound. Old stuff litters the staircase, and I have to be careful going down.

"Habibi!" my mother cries out when she sees me. She drops the stack of photos she was holding in her hands to rush up and take me in her arms.

I squeeze back, trying not to notice the new streak of gray atop her head.

"Look who it is!" my dad bellows happily before squeezing me as well. "Are you here to help?"

"Yep! Where should I start?" I put my hands on my hips and survey the scene around me. Most of the basement floor is covered in artifacts from several eras of Campbell history.

Rather than give me something useful to do, my mom pulls me over to the table. "You have to see this."

She brandishes an unending stream of photos of her and my father from the year they met. "We're hot!"

I laugh. "You certainly are."

We continue looking through all our old photos, including a pile of yellowing portraits of my mom's family that she says were taken back in the "old country" (her words). We discover that if we tie a scarf around my head, I look exactly like my hajib-wearing great-great grandmother.

Eventually it's impossible to ignore how little we're actually accomplishing. They point me to a stack of stuff that evidently belongs to me, and instructs me to make two piles: a Keep Pile and a Trash Pile.

Most of it goes in the Trash Pile.

I sort through old art projects. Most of them I don't remember even making, like an old cloth with my handprint painted all over it. I press my hand down over one of them, marveling at how much I've grown. I feel as if I'm holding my hand flat against a window and my younger self is doing the same on the other side.

It's a rather perturbing vision, especially since *nostalgia* isn't something I particularly enjoy doing business with—as if nostalgia personified is shaking my hand saying, "Hi, nice to meet you, life is fleeting."

I place the cloth gently on the Trash Pile. It remains there all of two seconds before my mom sees it and picks it up to coo at. She doesn't remember when or where I made it either, yet she insists we keep it and I don't bother arguing.

The next distracting item is an old journal I had forgotten about until this very moment. I flip through it, reading old entries, fixating on the ones where I express my inner thoughts about the world around me. I realize there's grown a massive disconnect between who I was and who I am today. I suppose that's true for everyone.

It dawns on me: I actively try not to think about the future, and I evidently prefer not to contend with the past. I suppose that leaves me the present. I suppose that means I should make the most of it.

My thoughts are interrupted by my dad stubbing his toe on a box of VHS tapes.

"Remind me, why are you going through all this again?" I ask them.

"Your mother and I won't be here forever, Jane-y," my dad says, and the unexpectedly maudlin statement makes me drop my journal. He rushes to correct himself. "I don't mean *death*, though of course that's an inevitability as well. I mean, well..." he sighs. He's struggling to tell me something.

"We're putting the house up for sale," my mom says from the table (where she's still sorting pictures). She doesn't even look up when she says it, nor when my dad shoots her an exasperated look.

"What?"

"This is too big a house for two people, sweetheart. The upkeep is getting to be too much for your old man."

I blink hard. It makes sense, of course it does, but I'd be lying if I said a part of me didn't assume they'd always be here, in *this* house.

"Where will you go?" I ask.

"We don't know yet," my mom says. "We're looking at a few townhomes in cities with cheaper taxes."

"Or maybe we'll just move in with you!" my dad jokes.

I laugh at the thought of all three of us crammed into my little dining room.

We work away for the next few hours, until my dad drops what he's doing and yells, "Pizza?" even though we're only a few feet away from him.

Despite hours of work and filling both receptacles to the point of overflowing, the basement looks relatively unchanged from when I arrived.

Realizing this makes me tired. And hungry. "Yes!" I yell back.

True to form, the trees are in full bloom not even a week later. Two weeks later, everyone's already forgotten winter.

People at work won't shut up about the weather we're having. "Seventy-five and sunny? *For four days straight?*"

Of course, I love it too. Especially because the warm air makes my outings with Ben all the more enjoyable.

Since the day I confirmed his identity, we've gone out five times.

We always meet at the coffee shop, either conveniently at the end of one of my shifts or around five when he's off of work. Then, he takes me somewhere to eat, a new place every time. I offered once to pay for myself, since I don't hold a job for nothing, but Ben just looked at me and said, "Nonsense." Any indignation I showed at this chauvinistic display vanished when he rather quickly explained that he really doesn't mind, and since he's the one who always picks the place, he believes he should be the one to pay, and that if the role is ever reversed, he would be happy to let me take care of the bill—reminding me that that's exactly what we did the first time we went out.

I've confirmed something interesting.

Ben's life only mimics the story version when it comes to things I've actually written down and solidified: his physical features, his career, his personality. Things I merely *thought* do not apply.

For instance, I always imagined him as having as much an aversion to sugar as he does to Izzie's sugary personality, but that has yet to make it into the manuscript. I realized this after witnessing him chow down on a donut ice cream sandwich.

"What?" he had asked defensively when he caught me staring. "I work out."

That, I knew. That, I wrote down.

The fact that there are aspects of his personality unknown even to me leads to many similar surprises, though not unwelcome ones. I've started keeping track of them all in the "Americano" document, a new habit that occasionally feels just a tad grimy. Yet, I can't stop. Between that, keeping Casey and

Suze appraised of the situation, and compulsively logging all my interactions with Ben (dialogue and everything), I've become something of a stalker.

But when I'm with Ben, I don't feel like a stalker. Or an author. I just feel like a girl, trying not to look like a pig while eating a donut ice cream sandwich.

Another interesting thing I've established is that changes to the story do not affect him. Just as an experiment, I once added in a sentence about Ben having a mole on his left hand, a much easier location to spot than his shoulder, but days went by and the mole never showed.

Casey and Suze have yet to officially meet him, a fact they won't let me forget.

Perhaps that is why they show up on Tuesday afternoon, work computers in tow. They know Ben is meeting me here at 5 for happy hour (my idea, my treat).

I shake my head at them. "Couple of punks."

Casey places a hand on her chest in mock offense. "Does Martha know how you treat your customers?"

They order separately, and I get to work making Casey and Suze's iced mocha and hazelnut latte, respectively, while they plug their computers into a wall socket at the same table they were at when they first saw Ben with their own eyes. Before we really knew who he was.

I slide a scone they didn't order onto their table as well. "You didn't get this from me," I utter under my breath.

The day ticks on, the tips suck, mopping the backroom makes me sweat (which is exactly why I shoved a clean shirt into my bag before leaving for work), but five o'clock eventually arrives.

Even though we just closed, Casey and Suze loiter with their bags packed while I finish setting up for tomorrow's shift.

When Ben finally arrives, he's greeted by three female heads swiveling to take him in. For a split second, he looks almost fearful. I stifle a laugh.

"Ben, these are my roommates, Casey and Suze." I point to each of them as I say their name.

"Oh, it's nice to meet you! I'm Ben." He actually shakes their hands.

Casey and Suze are smiling too much. If it makes Ben as uncomfortable as it makes me, he doesn't show it.

"Well, I'm all done here. I'm just going to use the bathroom before we go." I grab my shirt on the way, a light V-neck sweater that shows off my collarbone.

By the time I get back, Casey and Suze are laughing at something Ben said. Whatever it was, he seems pleased with himself.

"Would you like to join us?" Ben asks them, and I panic—not because I don't want them to come, but because I can't afford to buy drinks for all four of us. Much to my relief, Ben adds, "On me!"

Casey and Suze are well and truly charmed. They quickly agree, and we all pile into my car to go to the bar I originally had in mind, a trendy place famous for their inventive craft cocktails.

Happy hour drinks lead to more drinks, which eventually leads to dinner. The whole time, I marvel at the way Ben makes himself at home in our little group. Looks like Casey and Suze aren't the only ones getting a little charmed.

Over dessert, we tell him about Suze's family's cabin up north and how many trips we've made up there together. "We even have one coming up in…" Casey counts her fingers, "a week!"

"You should come!" Suze suddenly exclaims to Ben, surprising the entire table.

"Oh, no. I couldn't disrupt girl time! Some things must remain sacred."

"No, no, my friend and her husband are coming too, it'll be fun! We need another guy to join our party. Besides, it's a holiday weekend!"

Ben looks at me, clearly torn. If all he needs is a little push… "You should. When was the last time you took a vacation?"

"Good point. Okay, I'm in!"

Casey and Suze both cheer. I grin. Normally cabin trips are my prime time to catch up on writing, but this is even better. My writing is quite literally coming with us.

Next Friday can't come soon enough.

EIGHT

"It's times like these when you really wish you owned a minivan," says Suze's friend Manda rather forlornly.

The gang is gathered in front of our apartment, and none of us want to decide who goes in which of the two cars our numbers require.

"Wait, whose cars are we taking again?" asks Cameron, Manda's husband.

I met Manda and Cam when they were already together and swearing up and down that they were it for each other. Despite the ripe ages of twenty-three, they've been married for almost three years. I was invited to their wedding, even though the biggest thing linking us is Suze. I can tell it's the same thing with Casey. Still, we get along just fine.

Sometimes, I'm ashamed to admit, Casey and I gossip about how long their marriage will last. I mean, they tied the knot between their sophomore and junior years of college. Younger than I am now. I can't imagine marrying *anyone* right now, let alone having been married for two years. In my mind, marriage is still very much a vague, far off notion. Like, sure, eventually, when I'm a *real* grown up. But here are two people barely a year older than me, sharing their bank accounts and talking about buying their first home.

"I think we're taking mine," says Suze, "and yours?" she asks Cameron.

He pulls a face. "Ooh, I don't know if ol' Bessy can handle the trip." We all look over to his beat-up sedan. I guess when you're house-hunting, there's not much room for vehicle upgrades.

"I can drive, if that helps," Ben offers, and despite the many Minnesotan *"are you sure?"*'s, it's settled. Suze, Manda, and Cam in one car; Casey, Ben, and me in the other.

It takes another half an hour to split up the supplies to the two cars: a big cooler, a medium cooler, two cases of Cam's special craft beers that he can't get up north, three bags of Manda's organic snacks that *she* can't get up north, and all of our luggage (Casey and Suze are serial over packers). Then we decide whether to grab a bite now or on the road ("on the road" wins by two points).

Finally, we pack ourselves into our assigned vehicles and begin heading north, along with the rest of Minneapolis.

I'm in the front seat, Casey's stretched out in the back, already with her earbuds in. When I turn around to look at her, she gestures to her phone. I look down to see a text from her. Very smooth.

Does he have a fancy car like this in the book?

Yes, I type back. *Just like this.*

HMMMM.

I look at her and roll my eyes.

"You know you have about as much subtlety as a drama major, right?"

"Ouch!" I backhand his upper arm, which probably hurts me more than it hurts him.

In my peripheral vision, I can see Casey shake her head, turn her music up to an ungodly volume, and close her eyes.

"Do I even want to know what you two are texting about?"

That's a hard NO. "Don't you worry your pretty little head about it," I joke before realizing it could be read that as overt flirting.

To my relief, he doesn't get weird, only laughs.

"So," he changes the subject. "Navigator. DJ. You up for the challenge?"

"If by that you mean, 'make sure you remember the color of Suze's car in front of us and putting your phone on shuffle,' then yes."

He laughs and hands over his phone. I scroll through his playlists, selecting one conveniently labeled "Road trips," to start us off.

"You must go on a lot of road trips," I say, returning his phone to the center console.

"My family used to have a cabin up north, too."

"Used to?" This is new information to me. In my book, I never mention anything about any cabin, neither currently nor formerly in King Family use.

He nods but doesn't elaborate, and I get the distinct sense that he doesn't want me to ask any more about it. Perhaps it's the familial embarrassment I describe in my story.

I change the subject, asking instead how business is going.

"Really good, actually. I'm hoping to get promoted to Senior Editor by the end of the summer."

"That's awesome," I say, and I mean it. "I'm sure you're a shoe-in, especially since your family—" I clamp a hand over my mouth before I finish that sentence.

But I can see it's too late. Ben's gone rigid.

"How do you know about my family?" he asks in a low voice, presumably so Casey can't hear us over her music. I refrain from telling him we could be screaming and she wouldn't be able to hear us.

I'm at a loss for words. I can't try to make him think he brought them up himself because he didn't—and wouldn't, that much I know.

Thankfully, or rather, unthankfully, he fills in the gaps himself. "What, did you look me up? Want to make sure I was worth your time?"

Okay, whoa. I'm sensing some deep insecurities here that I have no prior knowledge of whatsoever. I guess you can write up the perfect man, and he'll still come out flawed.

"Ben, of course not. I don't care if your parents own a publishing company."

"Why did you look into it, then?"

"I didn't! I just…" *Quick, think of something like a lie but not a lie!* "I had already heard of King Publishing and when I saw your last name on my phone, I don't know, I just put two and two together."

His shoulders relax ever-so-slightly. Good. We're getting somewhere.

"How have you heard of King Publishing?" he asks, still uncertain. "I mean no offense by this, but you're a barista. Why are you keeping up with publishing companies at all?"

I inhale in a long, deep breath so I have a few extra seconds to think. I have to choose my words *very* carefully.

"Actually, I'm a writer. Well," I quickly correct myself, "I mean, I write. I don't know if you can call yourself a writer when you've only ever published short stories in your high school literary magazine."

Ben's eyebrows shoot up in surprise. "Really? I had no idea." His voice is back to normal. "What do you write?"

This is getting to be too weird. We're entering dangerous territory, but I can't turn back now. "Um, fiction. Stories. I've never finished anything. It's more of a hobby. I don't know if I'm any good at it."

"I'm sure you are. I'd love to read what you've got. I can give you some pointers if you want. I've learned nothing being a Managing Editor if not how to make a book sellable."

There's no way I will ever let Ben King read my story, though the weight of the offer is not lost on me. If it were anyone else...

"Thanks, I might take you up on that sometime!" My first outright lie. I will never in a million years take him up on that.

"No problem. And, for what it's worth, I think if you write, then you *are* a writer."

I turn to face him, and he meets my gaze for a couple seconds before turning back to the road. In those two seconds, all I saw in those brown eyes was warmth. It causes something to stir deep in my chest. I dismiss it before I can really consider what it is.

About an hour and a half into our four-hour journey, Cam texts the group chat to announce we're getting off at the next exit for dinner. He was one of the two who wanted to eat right away; the other was Manda. I feel bad for Suze having to drive with the two hungriest individuals of our group.

We follow Suze's car to a diner attached to a gas station. It doesn't look like much, but we usually stop here at least once on our trip. They have the best burgers.

Inside, we push two tables together and look over the menus, even though at least half of us already know what we want. All six of us end up ordering burgers in one form or another. Casey and I always split a cheeseburger with loads of extra pickles, Suze sticks with her plain burger sans sauce, Manda asks for a chicken sandwich without the bun, Cam gets a bacon burger with extra mayo, and Ben orders a double patty also with extra pickles. We get a few baskets of fries for the table.

"The best part of road-tripping, right here," Cam says, licking a drop of grease off his fingers. Manda wiggles her nose in disgust, using a fork and knife to cut into her chicken patty.

Casey and I are the first to clear our plates. "Do you think we should've gotten our own?" I ask, watching the rest of them chowing down.

"No!" she says, pointing a chastising finger. "We ask that every time, and every time we get another one we regret it. Wait ten minutes and you'll feel fuller."

Ben scoots his basket of fries towards me, and I gratefully accept a few. Casey's right, in ten minutes I feel just right. We pay at the counter to make it easy on our waitress, who remembers Casey, Suze, and I from our last trip.

Then we're on the road again. I watch the passing fields turn into dense wood, and when it gets dark, Suze flips on her beamers. Now is the time to be extra vigilant for deer, the cause of most vehicular accidents in Minnesota.

Finally, around nine p.m., we arrive at the cabin. We pull into the gravel driveway and climb out of our cars. It's a funny sight to behold—six people stretching in turn, like a strange alternative dance.

Suze walks up the porch to the front door using her phone as a flashlight. She unlocks the door and flips on the porch light and the entry light so we can see where we're going while we bring all our stuff inside.

Suze's family's cabin is a two-story log cabin sitting on what I personally believe is the clearest lake in all of Minnesota. I'm told the cabin itself used to be nothing special—more log than cabin—but now it's a finished three-bedroom, 2-bathroom structure with a full kitchen and everything. The grassy backyard leads right up to the water, where they have a private dock at which floats a large pontoon boat. They also have a canoe, tied up to a tree off to the side.

The only thing the cabin doesn't have is a beach. Just grass, then two feet of rocky bank, then water. This has never been an issue.

Manda and Cam, as the token couple, claim the lone basement bedroom, which leaves the upper two to the rest of us. One room has a bunk bed and a trundle; the other, a queen-sized bed with the oldest mattress known to man. Obviously, the girls and I take the room with the bunkbed.

When Ben tries to sit on his bed, he rolls to the side. I can't help but crack up at the sight.

"Sorry," Suze tells him. "We normally don't use that room if we can help it."

"It's okay," he laughs it off. "I'm sure it won't be a problem."

Once we're all settled into our respective rooms, we reconvene in the kitchen.

"Okay," Suze starts, taking the lead. "It's 9:45. The stores stay open until midnight. We can either go grocery shopping *now* and have everything we need for tomorrow's breakfast, or we can go in the morning and eat late."

The vote is unanimous: We go now.

Utilizing both cars to accommodate the lot of us, we break into two teams: Manda, Cam, and Suze are on food duty while the rest of us hit up the liquor store.

We stock up on beer, wine, hard apple ciders, and even some hard seltzers, though Manda's the only one who'll touch the stuff.

We meet the others in the one grocery store in town to find that they're only halfway done with our list, so we grab a second cart and split up within the store.

Tag-teaming results in acquiring everything we need quicker, just not as quick as we would if Casey didn't throw so many impulse purchases into our cart.

By the time we make it back to the cabin with two trunks full of food and drink, a new wave of hunger has washed over us. Manda and I quickly organize the groceries for a more seamless putting-away, and only when the perishables are in the fridge and the dry goods are in the cupboard do we determine the easiest thing to cook now.

Turns out, the least-involved meal we can do is mac n' cheese from a box. I make two, adding extra butter and a splash of milk to make it extra creamy.

No sooner do we gorge ourselves on all that dairy do we crash, all six of us visibly hitting a wall at the exact same time. We exchange a few "goodnights" before separating to our rooms for the night.

I'm out before I remember to set an alarm—and before I remember I don't need to. Such is life at the cabin.

NINE

It's nearly 10:30 when I rouse from a deep sleep, shocked at how late it is and slightly annoyed at Casey and Suze for not waking me up earlier.

Thankfully, I haven't missed breakfast. I know, because it's the smell of sizzling bacon that wakes me up.

Everyone's sprawled out in the kitchen/living room when I finally emerge from the room, still in my pajamas. A quick survey reveals I'm not the only one. Even Ben sits at the dining room table in a pair of flannel pajama pants and a black t-shirt. He's wearing black-framed reading glasses I certainly never gave him in my story, and he's bent over a thick paperback. His dark brown hair is slightly ruffled from sleep. *God, he's cute.*

Manda and Suze are duking it out for space in the small, U-shaped kitchen. From what I can tell, Suze is handling the classic staples (eggs, bacon, hash browns) while Manda multitasks several sweet brunch specialties (French toast, pancakes, and *oh my God, are those crepes?*). Manda is the breakfast queen.

"There's some coffee left if you want some," Cam calls out when he spots me, holding up his own mug as proof.

Yes, coffee. To reach the coffee pot, I must enter the kitchen. I do not accomplish this unscathed, as I pass the refrigerator at the exact moment Manda turns to grab something from it, resulting in an annoyed glance and an apology from me.

I empty the pot, and common decency dictates that I brew a fresh one, despite the fact that Suze and Manda would rather I leave their space immediately. I brew as fast as I can, taking a seat across from Ben at the table once I'm done.

He finally glances up from his book when I do. "Did you just get up?" he asks.

"What's it to you?" I mumble, blowing gently on my coffee.

He chuckles and shakes his head. "Well when did *you* get up, *Benjamin?*" I'm sassy this morning. Up until now, I've only ever used his full name in my head.

"If you must know, I've been up since six."

My jaw drops. I look wildly around me until Casey, a natural early riser, confirms this with a nod.

"But... but... you can't wake up that early at the cabin. It's sacrilegious!"

Ben just shakes his head and looks down at the table to hide his amused little side smile.

Eventually, Ben and I are ushered away from the table so Suze and Manda can set it. They place everything down aesthetically, and before the rest of us are allowed to take our place, Suze gets up on a chair to take several overhead snapshots. I'll admit: the table is quite a sight to behold. Manda even went so far as to make a little crepe station on a serving board, fitted with little round bowls of whipped cream, Nutella, strawberries, bananas, and some kind of berry puree.

Clean-up is going to be absolutely brutal.

For now, we gather around and dig in, passing around plates, a mimosa pitcher, the coffee pot. It's the kind of Homestyle brunch you only ever see in movies, something I make sure to express to Manda and Suze. Everyone gushes at their handiwork, and appreciation is verbalized from each of us throughout the entire meal.

Finally, when every platter, every dish, every jug has been cleared off and emptied out, we all sit back in our chairs and just talk. It seems no one wants to be the first to use the D-word (*dishes*).

We make a rough plan for the day. Since it's sunny and warm, we'll take the pontoon out. Usually that means hanging out on the water until dinner, so I'll have to remind myself to bring my book.

Suze and Manda dismiss themselves first, since cooking automatically disqualifies them from cleaning. Manda goes downstairs to shower and Suze does the same upstairs, leaving the rest of us to make a game plan.

Casey and I tackle the dishes, cleaning by hand whatever doesn't fit into the dishwasher, while the guys clear off the table and wipe down the counters.

The worst part isn't the dishes, it's the waiting for bathroom time. I think I'm the last to get in, and I already know there's no point in showering at this point; all the hot water will have been used up by now. Instead, I wash my face at the sink, apply a thick layer of sunscreen, followed by some concealer and mascara. I brush my teeth thoroughly to get rid of the lingering coffee breath, and then I pull on a pair of linen shorts and a sweatshirt, as it's always chillier out on the lake this time of year.

Everyone is already on the dock by the time I'm actually ready to go. The pontoon's cover sits off to the side, and Casey and Suze are currently squashing any spiders that dared make a home here in our absence.

Ben and Cameron lift the large cooler full of beer and ice into the boat carefully, setting it off the one side.

There's plenty of seating, so we all spread out, then Suze is putting the key in the ignition and waking the engine. She backs us out from the dock until the water is deep enough to submerge the propellers, then she's going full speed towards the center of the lake. I watch the bottom of the lake as we go. It's so clear, the lakebed doesn't disappear from sight until we're well off from the dock.

The air feels amazing. Something about the warm sun on your face paired with the cool wind in your hair makes you feel invincible.

At some point, Suze cuts the engine, and then the party begins. Beers are passed around, music is blared, and swimming is briefly discussed (though no one makes a move to do so).

We all take turns laying out on the flat surface at the very back of the pontoon, the best spot for sunning. When it's my turn, I plug in my earphones and spread out on my stomach, then my back. When my turn's up, I return to the chair at the front of the boat, where Ben looks up from his book and dips his head to peer at me over the rim of his sunglasses. "Did you just get a tan in half an hour?"

I look down to see that my arms have, in fact, grown a slight shade darker. "I guess I did." Such are the perks of being half Arab.

"It's just not fair." Manda's shaking her head, holding out her own arms, which are about as light as Cam's are dark. Opposite ends of the color spectrum.

The only thing breaking up our day are stops at the cabin to use the bathroom or freshen up on snacks until evening falls over the lake and we dock for the day.

I volunteer to make dinner, settling on spaghetti because it's easy. I take point while Casey acts as my sous chef, chopping what I need chopped and measuring out ingredients. We even mash some oil and a bunch of garlic on the inside of a couple loaves of French bread, baking it until the whole county can probably smell that someone's making garlic bread.

This time, we serve up the food buffet-style. Suze pops open a bottle of red wine and a bottle of white, and then we return to our places around the table to engage in more lively dinner discussion, especially when Ben asks Cameron and Manda how long they've been married.

"And you're… how old?" If Ben's trying to ask politely, he fails miserably. His tone is full of skepticism, and I brace myself for awkward silence.

To their credit, neither of the people in question seem to mind at all. "Twenty-three!" Manda shouts to the ceiling, arms raised. "We are twenty-three!"

"Listen," Cam starts, but he's laughing. He's loving this—either the attention or the opportunity to talk about the love of his life, I don't know. Maybe both. "We know, *we know* it's crazy. We know we were probably too young. But we also knew it would happen eventually, so we figured, 'why wait for the inevitable?'" He pours himself another glass of wine. "The tax breaks don't hurt either, huh babe?" He grins at his wife seated next to him, who rolls her eyes and throws a noodle at his face. It sticks to his forehead, and the table breaks into a chorus of loud laughter.

When we've finished eating, we leave the dishes where they sit so we can go back out on the lake for the sunset.

It's a magnificent sight to behold. As soon as the sun dips below the horizon, orange light explodes in all directions, spreading beams of light as far as it can reach.

We watch in silent awe, and don't return until dark.

We end the day with a bonfire out back, s'mores and all.

I rise a tad earlier on Sunday, yet I'm still the last one up.

The upper bathroom is occupied when I step out, and suspiciously silent.

"Don't bother," Suze says from the kitchen where she's making exactly one breakfast sandwich. I guess today is a free-for-all. "Casey's been in there all morning."

I groan. I hop downstairs to the use the secondary bathroom and nearly crash into Ben at the base of the stairs. "Whoa," he says, catching me by the upper arms. I look up at him and start a little when I realize how close we are.

He quickly releases me and I take a generous step back, rubbing at the back of my neck nervously. "Sorry," I murmur before skirting quickly around him and locking myself in the bathroom.

Leaning against the door, I place a hand gently over my chest to feel my heart nearly beating out of it. *Calm down, Jane. Calm the heck down.*

I don't know what's going on, but whatever it is, I fear it.

When I return upstairs, I claim a seat on the floor, even though there's plenty of space next to Ben on the couch. He looks at me strangely for a split second before returning his focus to his book.

Finally, Casey emerges from the bathroom, giggling. "Guys, I think I'm high on fumes."

We all gape at her. She went into the bathroom a brunette, and came out a blonde.

"What the—" I say at the same exact time Cam says, "Oh snap!" and Suze says, "Dude!" Ben and Manda just stare.

A strong puff of chemicals bleeds into the air shortly thereafter, and we all start making choking noises. "Jesus, Case!" Suze waves a hand furiously in front of her. "You should've at least used the fan!"

"Sorry," she giggles again before making herself something to eat. The rest of us resort to opening all the windows to air it out, but even that isn't enough. We end up in the grassy backyard where Ben and Cam, beers in hand, kick around a soccer ball while the girls and I lounge on a giant picnic blanket, nursing a large jug of sangria.

Two drinks in, I start to get a little restless. I sit up and survey the landscape until my eyes land on the canoe. "Does anyone want to go canoeing with me?"

"I will." I look up to see Ben approach. His game or whatever with Cam seems to be over with.

"Okay, sweet." *'Sweet'? What are you, twelve?*

Ben unties it from the tree while I use my flip-flop to attack the swarm of daddy long legs materializing after we flip it over.

Sliding it into the water is easy enough; what's not easy is managing to get both of us inside without drenching our ankles. We manage this by Ben first holding the canoe from the shore while I climb to the back, trying not to fall over when it wobbles

99

underneath me, and then Ben simultaneously jumping in while pushing us off from the shore. We each take a paddle and start rowing, me taking up the lead while Ben powers the canoe from the back.

I know exactly where to go, so I instruct Ben over my shoulder to follow my lead. We stay mostly close to the shore, floating through patches of wetland rushes until eventually arriving at a little opening in the brush—a narrow passageway to another lake.

"Ooh," I hear him say behind me, his voice full of wonder. I'm glad he can't see how big my smile is.

We go slowly through the passage, bumping into the edges and sometimes getting stuck on an especially shallow part. We even glide under a little bridge from the street. I try not to look up at all the spider webs above.

Then, suddenly, we're on a completely different lake. There are no cabins here. It's entirely surrounded by trees, and much smaller than the one we just came from. Also unlike the lake Suze's family's cabin sits on: this one is covered in lily pads. Lily pads *everywhere*.

Cartoons I used to watch as a kid had me believing I'd see frogs chilling out on top of these lily pads eventually, but I've yet to witness this phenomenon myself. As far as I know, their only purpose is to serve as landing pads for dragonflies.

"I wish I could lay out on a lily pad," I find myself saying out loud.

"Me too," Ben says.

We stop rowing, and the gentle breeze carries us wherever it so pleases. I turn around on my bench so we're facing one another, but quickly realize I have nothing to say. Ben's quiet, too. Instead, when the breeze pushes us closer to the shallow perimeter, I lean over the canoe's edge to peer down into the water.

It never fails to surprise me how many fish are actually swimming below us. All you need to do is focus on one little minnow and then suddenly you're seeing a whole swarm of them. Stranger, still, is that once you see it, you can't *un*-see it.

I poke the water to scare them but only a couple fish scatter. The first one I spotted doesn't budge.

Then I look at the lily pads, the sky, anything but Ben. I notice a few clouds rolling in, some darker than others.

"You're acting kind of weird."

"I am?" I play dumb, ignoring the twinge of irritation I feel at him for calling me out.

"Yes. Care to explain?"

"Not really."

"If I did something…"

I sigh, finally raising my eyes to meet his. "You didn't. It's just, I don't know, I'm in a mood. I can't place it." That much is true.

"I can understand that." He looks off to the side, exposing a chiseled jawline and strong throat. Like a Roman statue.

That's it, I wrote him to be way too hot.

"Actually," he continues, "sometimes I feel like I don't really know myself."

I inhale sharply. Is he getting self-aware? "What do you mean?"

"I mean, I have this idea of myself in my head, and I often find myself doing something inconsistent with that idea." He rubs his face. "That's not a good way of describing it. Ugh, I don't even know what I'm saying."

Haven't I thought the exact same thing? The Ben in front of me regularly breaks out of the mold of his literary self. I suppose I shouldn't be surprised he feels this way, but I am. Ben—this Ben—is just so painfully *real*.

"Forget the idea you have in your head," I earnestly tell him. "You are your own person. Everything you do makes you that person."

His face is open, his eyes hopeful. "You think so?"

I wish I could take his face in my hands. Instead, from across the canoe, I say, "Yes, I really do." I can tell he believes me.

Does what I think matter to him? Do *I* matter to him?

Plop. A fat raindrop lands right on Ben's forehead, and we look at each other wide-eyed before quickly lowering our paddles into the water and heading back in the direction from which we came.

The rain is already over by the time we crash into the shore, but it's too late. We're both soaking wet. We pull the canoe ashore and then take in our mutual state.

He looks at me.

I look at him.

Then we burst out laughing.

TEN

The wildlife here demands to be heard—*especially* after a rain.

Though the window is sealed shut, it sounds as if a choir of a million frogs is performing right in my room, rendering sleep impossible.

I kick off my covers and make my way quietly to the kitchen, selecting a beer from the fridge.

Only when I've plopped myself down at the end of the dock do I realize I forgot a bottle opener, and this isn't a twist-off. I place it to the side and pull my knees to my chest to block out the brisk breeze.

Nights like these only exist up north.

In the city, cool summer nights are rare, with the humidity normally carrying right on into the next day. It can be stifling.

But here, between the breeze and the darkness, even the mosquitos can't find me.

The sky is incredibly clear, revealing a shocking array of stars. Have there always been this many stars?

I feel the dock sway and turn to see a dark figure approaching, their identity a mystery under the cover of darkness. It's not until he's right in front of me do I realize it's Ben. He plops down beside me with, not a beer, but an entire bottle of red wine, already opened. In his other hand are two plastic cups folded between his fingers.

"I don't know how the rest of them sleep with all this noise," he says before spotting the beer. "Looks like we had the same idea."

"Ah, but *you* came prepared," I reply, plucking one of the plastic cups from his grasp, "whereas *I* forgot the stupid opener." I hold out the cup and he pours generously.

The wine is lukewarm and smooth, sliding down my throat with such ease. Warmth spreads in my body from the inside out.

We sit cross-legged like this for a while: no talking, just staring out over the vast, dark lake, sipping our wine. It's a scene so perfect I never would've been able to come up with one like it without first experiencing it for myself.

When I get close to finishing a cup, Ben fills it. When he knocks back his, I'm on stand-by with the bottle.

Sometimes I forget how alcohol works. It seems silly that I could have two screwdrivers with breakfast this morning and feel nothing yet exactly three cups of grape juice has my brain feeling all sorts of fuzzy.

I suppose I also haven't eaten a thing since dinner several hours ago, and even then it was only fish. Barely any handy dandy carbs to soak up the booze. *Oh who cares, Ja-ane?* I giggle. *I am hi-larious.*

"That you are," Ben says good-humoredly.

I guess I said that last part out loud. I should be more careful. *Wouldn't want any deep dark secrets coming out, now would we?*

"What deep dark secrets?"

Crap.

I turn my face to peer at Ben, noting the slight lag in my vision, like my eyeballs are just one beat behind the rest of my body. Heavy behind my eyelids.

He meets my scrutiny head-on, blinking lazily. I guess I'm not the only one feeling the effects of our shared cabernet.

"Trust me, you don't want to know." I giggle again. Everything is just so *funny.*

"Oh, but I *do*, Jane." He leans in a little, and it takes everything in me not to clutch my chest like a Victorian puritan.

"I want to know everything about you. And why I can't seem to stop thinking about you."

My breath catches. I'm not laughing anymore.

Ben's eyes, too, seem to have regained some focus as he stares into mine. "What is it about you?"

It's no surprise that I feel a pull every time I'm around him. What is surprising is that he would be equally drawn to me. It makes so much sense. So much troubling, twisted, wonderful sense.

"Jane," he says again, softer this time, and I return to the present.

To the cool breeze pushing us closer, to the empty bottle of wine egging me on, to the man next to me who I'm tragically half in love with already.

For once, I don't think. I just lean forward and kiss him.

I pull away almost as soon as our lips touch to see his reaction. His eyes are darker than ever, so dark I can't see his pupils—and intense. So very intense. He stares at me for a beat too long, just long enough for regret to seep in around the edges of my consciousness, when suddenly he kisses me back.

Unlike my kiss, soft and quick, his is deep, unending. He presses his hands against my back and pulls me closer, and I let my hands find his face, tracing his jawline indulgently.

Until he covers my hand with his, and gently pulls it away.

I lean back to frown at him, blinking slowly until I see his expression for what it is. He's unsure, he's conflicted, he's sorry. That last one is especially disappointing.

Still, I flash him a small smile to let him know it's okay.

I sigh tiredly, laying down until my back is flat on the dock. Ben does the same beside me, and we gaze up at the stars, the ones we <u>ever</u> see in the city, neither of us saying anything.

I fold my hands over my stomach, and warmth spreads from my belly, making me sleepy. Or maybe it's just the wine.

Maybe it was all just the wine.

I'm awoken by light so blinding I see it first though my eyelids. I try to ignore it, to will it away. But the sunrise can't be stopped.

Sunrise.

My eyes bolt open. I see now why I didn't want to be disturbed by the sun. I'm curled into Ben's chest, still on the dock, more of a warming mechanism than a romantic one, and his arms are wrapped around me probably for the same reason.

I squeeze my eyes shut again. It takes some effort, but eventually I remember the hazy events that led us here.

The wine. The kissing. The stargazing.

I don't exactly remember how long the latter lasted, but it's obvious that eventually we both fell asleep exactly as we were, side by side on the cold wooden dock.

And now, sunrise.

I sit up slowly, head pounding. Ben's arms drop lazily from my side, but he doesn't stir.

Logically I know I should wake Ben and stumble back up the cabin to drink a gallon of water each, but the sunrise is too tempting. I wake up before the sunrise three times a week, but I never get to enjoy it.

It's the sunset in reverse, but somehow cleaner, crisper. There's no anticipation in a sunset; you just watch until it's gone and then you go inside. But the sunrise...

The beams of light, the thing that woke me up, arrive first. A runway for the star of the show. The tip of the sun peaks over the horizon, and it's exhilarating. *She's coming. She's almost here. There she is. She isn't alone. She brought a new day with her.*

I glance down at the sleeping form beside me. A deep ache spreads inside my chest at the sight of him.

It just isn't fair. He's only had a month to get to know me, whereas I've had actual years to fall in love with him.

But I can't be. I shouldn't be. Just like Suze said, there's a power imbalance here that just isn't fair to him.

Maybe I should come clean. Try to explain calmly and logically what can't be calmly or logically explained. He might be upset at first. He might even flatly deny it. But eventually he'd have to acknowledge it's the red yarn around our pinkies, inextricably linking us together.

Great, now I'm bargaining.

No, I can never tell him.

I bury my face in my hands, defeated. I can't avoid him, and I can't be with him in the way I want to be. What does that leave me?

"You're the most tragic girl in the world," I sigh to myself.

"Hnng?"

I pull my hands away from my face and turn just in time to see Ben rising groggily. His forehead is crinkled in a deep frown as he takes in the scene. The sun, me.

I watch him go through the same mental slideshow I did. I can tell the moment he remembers the kiss, because he looks down to his right, eyebrows ever-so-slightly raised. It's a scandalous expression, and I stifle a laugh.

His eyes flick to me, and he smiles too. I try to read the smile—Contentment? Happiness? Guilt?—to no avail.

It would appear he simply doesn't want to talk about it.

I suppose I don't, either.

"How was the sunrise?" he asks hoarsely.

110

"Perfect," I reply. "It was absolutely perfect."

We both know I'm not talking about the sunrise.

ELEVEN

Casey—I still can't get used to the blonde hair—rubs her eyes when she sees me sprawled out on the couch, Ben brewing a pot of coffee in the kitchen. Despite my best efforts, I couldn't fall back asleep, and at this point, it doesn't seem to matter. I can sleep on the drive home.

Casey gives me a look, like *"should I ask?"* and I shake my head quickly. She nods understandingly.

She yawns loudly instead. "Make coffee faster," she grumbles to Ben, and I'm grateful to my friend for breaking the tension.

"Yes, ma'am."

Slowly, one by one, the rest of the gang appear, sleep in their eyes. So this is what it's like to be the first one up. Already two cups of coffee down, I feel like I have an edge over the rest of them. I start cracking a bunch of eggs in a bowl to scramble for everyone, and Ben wordlessly joins, peeling open a fresh packet of bacon and fishing the griddle out of the dishwasher.

We decide over breakfast to take the boat out one more time before we pack everything up for the drive home, so when we're done eating, that's what we do.

It's by far the nicest day yet, not a single cloud in the sky. This time, we do swim, jumping off the highest points of the pontoon into the blue water below. The noon sun warms the water's surface but leaves everything beneath cold as ice, making for quite the shock to our systems, but we keep it up for hours. We all agree that we're not ready to leave.

Eventually, though, we have to admit that we're running out of daylight, and we still need to pack and clean up after ourselves.

Later, once the pontoon is securely tied to the dock and the cabin is sufficiently wiped clean of our presence, it's time to go home.

We split up into the same groups of three as before, driving off from the cabin just as the sun begins to set. Just as I predicted, a wave of drowsiness hits me once we're on the highway. I fold my arms and sink back into my seat, closing my eyes.

* * *

After all the goodbye hugs and thanking Suze and Ben for offering up their vehicles, I'm tucked safely in my room, finally alone with my laptop.

I have a lot of writing to catch up on.

The best thing to distract me from what happened: writing about what happened. The words flow easily as I commit to paper everything that was said and done this weekend— everything I can remember, anyway, filling in the blanks with my own narrative.

I describe how the hazy kiss made me feel in the moment, my inner conflict when I put a name to said feelings, and Ben's distractedness for the rest of the day. It's cathartic.

It also makes it easier to ignore Casey and Suze taking turns peeking their head around my foldable wall, waiting for me to take a break from my typing so that they can ask the inevitable. I fully plan on telling them everything; I just have to tell my keyboard, first.

When I'm all caught up, I hit save and close down my laptop. Though it's late, the girls are still in the living room. They perk up when I shuffle around the foldable wall, bounce in their seats while I plop into the chair and curl my legs under me, and lean so far off the couch when I look at them I think they're going to fall off.

I cover my face with my hands. "We kissed."

That's when they start screaming.

"How was the cabin?" Danny asks over his avocado toast the following day. It's the time of morning when it's acceptable to pop a squat with a friend for a few minutes, and besides, we're at the table closest to the espresso bar, so if a customer comes in I can easily hop into action.

"Oodles and oodles of fun, as always." He rolls his eyes. "Suze's married friends were there too, and they're pretty fun."

"The couple who got married when they were, like, twenty?"

I shake my head in awe. "That brain, I swear." He shrugs, like, *what can ya do?"*

"Yeah, and there were crepes, and some swimming, a lot of drinking…"

I'm stalling. It feels weird to deliberately erase Ben from the attendance list, but Martha's words fill my head. No, no. I remind myself that I didn't—*don't*—believe what she said to be true. "Oh, and Ben was there, too."

Danny stops chewing. Looks up at me. "Meet-Cute Guy?"

An actual snort escapes me. "'*Meet-Cute Guy*'?"

He drops his toast down on his plate mock-confrontationally, and I'm glad. His very reaction to Ben's presence at the cabin proves that Martha was wrong—or just pulling a cruel joke.

"Correct me if I'm wrong, *Jane*, but isn't spilling your drink on someone considered a meet-cute?"

"I'm just more surprised that you know the term 'meet-cute'."

He scoffs, still playing offended. "Typecasting me as the dumb jock, are we?"

I shake my head in amazement. "Danny P., *what*—"

"I watch a lot of movies, okay?" he exclaims. "Now stop deflecting! Tell me about Meet-Cute Guy."

"It wasn't a meet-cute. I already knew him before I spilled coffee on him." My words are broken up by my own chuckling. I can't stop imagining Danny curled up on the couch watching *The Holiday* and learning the term "meet-cute" for the very first time, as I did many years ago.

"What?" he demands, but he's laughing too.

I realize he's probably more curious about the capacity in which Ben came along to the cabin. "Anyway, Suze invited him to the cabin."

"Suze is the one who invited him," he repeats, puzzled. I get the sense that there's a different question, hidden just beneath the surface.

"I mean, he and I have been hanging out a bit over the last few weeks, but yeah, it was Suze's idea to invite him to the cabin."

"Ahh." He still looks confused. And maybe just a little unsettled. He doesn't ask anything else.

I open my mouth to ask him about his weekend, since a Danny P. vacation story is exactly the thing to push us out of one of our rare awkward moments when the bell over the door chimes, and we both look up to see Meet-Cute Guy himself strolling in, looking for me.

I look at Danny. "I'll be right back..." My voice trails off, and I hate how obvious I am. I would've been better off saying, "see ya never!"

"Yeah, go," he waves me away. "I should get going, anyway. I'll see you later."

"See ya," I say, watching him pass by Ben without looking at him. Ben, however, watches him with a curious expression on his face.

"Hey," I say as soon as I reach the counter. "Do you want your Americano?"

He blinks, shaking away whatever thought just popped into his head. Oh to be a little nerve ending in that brain of his. "Um, yeah, sure, but I also..." He lowers his voice. "Listen, I'm sorry for being so weird after… Anyway, can we talk later? There's something I want to say."

"There is?" I ask hopefully.

He nods, smiles. "There is. See, I was thinking—"

The door chimes with a new customer, and Ben glances up at the sound, freezing midsentence. He pulls a double-take, and I turn to see what's disrupted our precious moment.

My eyes go wide. It's not a *what*, but a *who.*

This time, I'm not holding hot coffee. If I was, I would've dropped it.

She's here.

In Common Ground.

Isabel Archer.

TWELVE

It's like a slow-motion entrance from a movie. There she is, curly shoulder-length hair and all, strolling confidently to the counter and smiling at me like this isn't her first time here.

"Hi!" she greets me brightly, ignoring Ben beside her who, oh, by the way, won't stop staring. "Can I get one of those mocha Frappuccino thingies? I've got a major hankering for something sweet and chocolatey."

I nod wordlessly, like a stupid little idiot. The only thing that comes out of my mouth is her total, and she hands over a few bills, still smiling. She leans on the counter and glances all around her, full of childlike wonder. "I love the aesthetic in here. Very Parisian."

This gets a laugh out of me, albeit a short one. "My boss will love that."

I get to work on her Frappuccino, pulling out the blender and measuring out ingredients as fast as I can. The sooner she gets her beverage, the sooner Ben's attention goes back to me. The sooner he finishes his sentence. *"I was thinking..."*

I've never wanted to know the ending of a sentence more.

"Do you guys ever feature local art in here?" she continues, oblivious, still looking around. She catches Ben looking and he quickly turns away. *Very smooth, Benjamin.*

"Sometimes," I say while I lock the blender in the place. It takes a few tries, since it's a finicky mechanism even when I'm not rushing. I flip the blender on, rendering it impossible for Izzie to say anything else, as I'm pretty sure I know where this is going.

"I would love to hang my work up in here." There it is. "I'm Izzie Archer, by the way. Well, Isabel, but only my grandmother calls me that."

Huh. Confirming Izzie's identity was way easier than confirming Ben's. A breeze, even.

It doesn't feel like a revelation so much as a punch to the gut.

Ben's ears perk at the sound of her name, and he turns to face her. The worst part? I knew he would.

"Your parents must be Henry James fans," he says, impressed.

She looks at him with a blank expression on her face. This, too, doesn't surprise me.

He cocks his head to the side and repeats himself, even though I know his words fall on deaf ears. "Henry James… You know, author of *The Portrait of a Lady*?" Still, nothing. "The book whose main character is named Isabel Archer?"

Izzie cracks a smile. "Oh!" Ben mistakes her exclamation for recognition, and relief flashes across his face until she adds: "What a weird coincidence!"

And there it is, written all over his face: Distaste. That's the Ben I know. That's the Ben I *wrote*.

He finally looks at me, baffled. "*You* know what I'm talking about, right?"

"Uh-huh," I squeak. *You have no idea how much I know.*

I witness their entire exchange wide-eyed, swinging my head left and right depending on who's talking. "Whip?" I finally ask Izzie.

"Of course!"

I fit the round lid to the cup and angle the whipped cream nozzle so I can fill the lid to maximum capacity. Ben raises his eyes judgmentally as I hand it over. This, Izzie instantly recognizes.

She ignores him, keeping her eyes almost determinately locked on me. "So what would I have to do to get my stuff in here?"

I want to tell her she can't, that Martha swore off local artists ever since one of them relentlessly hit on her, but it wouldn't be true. (Well, a local artist *did* hit on her. A man my age, no less. We started joking that she was becoming his muse. She asked him to take his art down shortly after.)

"You'd want to talk to the owner, Martha." I fish her card out from the drawer under the register and hand it to her.

She takes the card from my hand. "Thank you…"

It takes a second too long for me to realize she's waiting for my name. "Jane."

"… Jane. Thank you, Jane. I promise I'll be back!"

I force a smile, and then I feel bad for forcing it, so I force it some more. She doesn't notice, anyhow.

"Enjoy your hot bean water," she calls over her shoulder to Ben on her way out. Izzie: 1. Ben: 0.

As soon as she's out the door, Ben gives me a look, like, *Can you believe that?*

Yes, I can believe that. All too well.

"Anyway, you were saying?"

"Hmm?"

"You wanted to talk later…"

"Oh! Right. Yes. So you're free? Meet me for ramen when you're done with work?"

I deflate a little. Somehow, I doubt he'll be confessing his feelings to me over steaming bowls of noodles. I almost want to say no, but we can't just not talk about what happened between us. "Sounds good!" I put two thumbs up just for good measure, more to convince myself.

When he's gone, I slink to the backroom and shoot a quick text to the "Roomies" group chat. I type, *I'll be home a little late, but when I am, have a drink ready.*

After confirming when Ben will arrive at the ramen place, I wait inside Common Ground (now locked and dark) until five minutes after the time he gave me, just to be safe. I figure I may as well not be embarrassingly early for my own rebuffing.

I shuffle down the street towards the ramen joint. It's not too busy at this time of day, and I spot him right away at a small booth near the back. He smiles when I slide in across from him.

"How was work?" he asks distractedly, like he's only asking to be polite before he tells me about his.

I frown. "Nothing out of the ordinary. You?"

He leans in. "You'll never believe who I ran into at the company."

I purse my lips. Something tells me I'll have no problem believing who he ran into at the company.

"Isabel Archer, that crazy girl from before!" he bursts out.

We were supposed to talk about us. We were supposed to talk about the kiss. He was supposed to finish his sentence. *"I was thinking…"* Now that's pushed to the side, or maybe just plain forgotten. Not just by Ben, either.

Because, despite myself, I'm enthralled by what he tells me next.

In my story, Izzie submits a travel photography book proposal to King Publishing on a whim while she's in town, and to her surprise, it gets picked up. Her joy quickly sours when she realizes the rude (yet annoyingly handsome) man she met at the bookshop is the Managing Editor assigned to her book. For the next couple months, she and her editor exchange witty banter, argue over formatting and design concepts to no end, learn unexpected things about each other, and slowly but surely fall in love.

It's wild getting Ben's version of the *exact same story*.

Minus all the other stuff, of course. He's only just entered Act One territory, after all.

As he recounts the events of the last few hours, I'm surprised exactly once.

It happens after he complains about Isabel's outlining abilities. "I mean, God, the woman flies by the seat of her pants. Publishing is organized! How am I supposed to work with that?"

"Why don't you just ask to get reassigned?" I'm startled to hear myself ask. I realize it's a plot hole that's been nagging at me—if Ben can't stand Izzie that much at the beginning, why doesn't he use the pull he has as the CEO's son to get a different project? I could never come up with anything better than "because of underlying captivation with both Izzie and her antics, *duh*," but that's a little too cheesy, even for me, even writing chick-lit.

Ben seems significantly less thrown by my question than I was. I push my barely-touched ramen to the side, deeply invested in what he's about to say.

"I tried," he wails, "but my dad informed me not-so-subtly that if this project goes well, I'd be promoted to Senior Editor fair and square. I can't pass up that opportunity."

And I remember: Ben doesn't talk about his family at work. He keeps his head down and he gets the job done, no matter how lowly, proving his worth independent from his name.

He wants to rise through the ranks because he earns it, not because it's handed to him on a nepotistic silver platter.

So his potential promotion hinges on the success of Izzie's book. Genius! Couldn't have come up with something better myself, apparently.

"Does Izzie know your family owns the company?"

"Of course." He looks at me like I'm stupid. "That smug little face," he seethes to himself, presumably referring to Izzie's when she put two and two together.

Up until now, I've been able to follow along pretty seamlessly. Now we're getting into uncharted territory.

This is all wrong. In the book, Ben hides his last name from everyone at work, instead using his mother's surname. Izzie doesn't learn the truth until much later, when he finally takes her home to meet the family, and by home, I mean a sprawling family estate.

Izzie first noticed the gateman. Then, the gate. She glanced at Ben, but his face maintained his usual neutral expression. Unreadable, as always, save for the finger-tapping on the steering wheel—the one indication of nerves, she'd learned.

They winded through thick rows of trees until finally coming upon an opening. A very large opening. Ben cut the engine but didn't make a move to get out. Izzie took a cursory glance at the mansion before them, then unbuckled her seatbelt and swiveled to face him.

"And what, exactly, does your family do for work?"

In the book, Izzie puts two and two together the moment she sets eyes on the house, but by then, she's too deep in her feelings for Ben to give a rip that he kept it from her. She handles the news gracefully and doesn't think any less of him.

I can only imagine the kind of prejudice Izzie already has having discovered that he's the son of the company's CEO right off the bat. It's going to be harder for them to get together than I thought. Less enemies-to-lovers and more just... enemies.

Fine by me.

I know not to bring up the kiss tonight. Ben's already in a hell-raising mood over the whole Izzie debacle, and I'm not in the habit of bringing up left-field subjects.

But I do want to talk about it. I want to do more than talk about it. I want to do it again.

That can only happen if Izzie stays out of my way.

She may be a creation of mine, but that doesn't mean we have to be in each other's lives. It doesn't mean she has to be in Ben's life, more than what's necessary. I can break him out of the mold I've created, right? I can make sure he doesn't fall in love with Izzie.

I can get my own happily-ever-after, or whatever.

One I couldn't have written better myself... literally.

* * *

"I'm sorry, what?" Casey asks at the same time Suze inhales her Rosé, resulting in such a violent coughing fit that Casey and I have to take turns slapping her back.

I waited until we were at the nearest lake with a picnic blanket and a bottle of cheap Rosé split three ways to share the new developments.

"Isabel. The main character." Casey's gone still, like she's half expecting me to yell "GOTCHA!" and laugh in her face.

"Well, technically, they're both main characters. Third person, and all that."

"Whatever," she waves away the clarification. "This is getting crazy, Jane. I mean, think about what this implies. Does an entire company—King Publishing—now exist in the real world because of *you*? And what about their families! This goes way beyond two main characters."

My mouth falls open. I hadn't even thought about that.

"And all the people who know them and the company, are they made up too?" Suze wheezes, her throat still hoarse from all the coughing.

Casey looks at me like I'm an alien. Or a superhero. Or an alien superhero. "How much power do you have over our universe, Jane?"

"I dunno."

Suze looks over the rim of her Solo cup, deep in thought. "I wonder if you're the only one, or if this has happened to other people. Other writers."

I hadn't thought about that either. I lay on my back and throw the arm not attached to a Solo cup full of Rosé across my face dramatically. "You guys are freaking me out. I didn't sign up for all this reality-questioning garbage."

"Sorry," they sigh in tandem, stretching out beside me.

We're silent for a while, staring up at the dark, dusk sky, contemplating the meaning of life and the universe itself. At least, I am.

"Hey, what does this mean about the kiss?" Suze eventually asks.

"I'm not really sure," I reply quietly.

"What do you *want* it to mean?" Casey asks.

"I... I want this to mean nothing. I want Izzie to not be an issue. I want... I want *Ben*." My voice waivers pathetically, and I shake myself out of it before I go full on soap opera on my friends. "Ugh." I try to laugh, and my sad attempt is so hilarious I actually do laugh. I sit up to drink some Rosé. "Do you guys think I'm a perv?"

Casey chuckles. "Only a little! But we support you, girl!"

Suze chokes on her Rosé a second time, and Casey and I roll our eyes at each other before resuming the back-slapping.

THIRTEEN

On Wednesday, my day off, I sleep in knowing full well it'll ruin me for my opening shift tomorrow. Once the late morning sun hits my bed, I sit up in a huff and reach for my laptop.

When I glance again at the clock, it's nearly six p.m.

I peer at the clock, certain I'm in the beginning stages of far-sightedness, but no, it's really 5:46 *p.m.* Which means I spent the day immersed in my writing, and I definitely smell.

When had I plugged my laptop in? When did I take my bathroom breaks? Have I eaten?

I glance down at my laptop. I've spent the last however-many-hours compiling all the scenes I've written involving Ben—and now Izzie—and putting them in order under a new document, "Untitled II" (for lack of a better idea). Then I went through and added more dialogue, described settings in more detail, and added in some other events in between that didn't involve any literary characters come to life. It's almost become its own story at this point.

I rub my eyes long enough to see fireworks, then I push off my bed, grab some clean clothes, and make my way to the bathroom.

"You look like you just woke up," Casey says over her laptop as I pass the living room.

"I *feel* like I just woke up." I stop, look around groggily. "Where's Suze?"

"She had to go in to work today." She looks at me sideways. "You didn't notice?"

"Nuh-uh." I catch a whiff of my own B.O. and quickly continue on my way, wondering how I failed to notice it all this time.

After a long, warm shower and some decadent skin care, I feel good as new. And starving. I go back to my room to see what I can order for delivery when I see a text from Danny from three hours ago. *Pizza 2nite? Been a minute.*

Pizza sounds amazing. And I know he's talking about the fancy flatbread place not even a five minute walk from my apartment. It's practically in our backyard.

I quickly text back, *Pizza! Pizza! Yes! Is it too late???*

I see the three little dots pop up almost immediately. *It's never too late for pizza, Jane.*

Huzzah! Meet there in twenty minutes?

Absolutely.

As much as I hate to disrupt the products I've lathered generously on my face following my shower, I cover it with some light makeup and change from my clean sweats into some clean clothes. Linen shorts, because it's finally warm enough, and a loose-fitting t-shirt. Casey watches with a curious expression on her face as I pull on a pair of sneakers by the front door. "Got a hot date?"

"Hot, yes; but date, no." I realize my Freudian slip as soon as the words leave my mouth, but it's too late to take them back.

Casey nods. "I still can't believe you made out with that fine specimen."

Confusion clouds my brain for a fraction of a second until it hits me. "Oh, no, I'm meeting Danny P."

She leans forward in her seat. "*Oh?* Another *hottie with a body?*"

I roll my eyes. "Whatever. You know Danny P. and me are strictly buds."

"Ha. *Bud-zoned.*"

"'*Bud-zoned*'?" I laugh, but internally I'm thinking, *Oh no, not this "Poor Danny P." thing again.*

132

Thankfully, Casey only laughs at her own genius and returns to whatever's on her laptop screen (possibly work but more likely *Gilmore Girls*). "Have fun," she sing-songs.

I roll my eyes on the way out.

It's a beautiful evening, warm with a cool breeze and very little humidity—probably the last of its kind—so we opt to sit out on the patio after we've ordered our pizzas at the front counter.

"Do you ever notice how counter service has taken over the food industry?" I ask, simply because Danny always has something to say about everything and it's fun to get him going. At least, it is until he talks so much you can't get a word in edgewise, but we've got to get the conversational ball rolling, somehow.

"I know right?" he says excitedly, and a close-mouthed smile spreads across my face at my one-woman inside joke. "It's like sit-down restaurants are a thing of the past."

"Why is that, do you think?" I take a sip from my soda glass and watch him like he's a subject in a lab. *Fascinating, just fascinating.*

"I know what you're doing," he says conspiratorially.

"What am I doing?" I feign innocence.

"You're trying to get me to rant. Well guess what Ja-ane, it ain't gonna work. I'm all tapped out."

So I guess he is in on the joke. "Tapped out?"

He shakes his head. "Just a long day."

"Long as in bad?"

"Long as in… I didn't start my day with a *de-luxe* Common Ground latte." There he goes again with the unnecessary syllable-adding.

"Ahh. Didn't have time?"

"I never go on Wednesdays," he answers casually.

"You don't?" I suppose I wouldn't know that, since I tend not to spend more time at my job than absolutely necessary, no matter how aesthetically pleasing it may be. "Why, is it because I'm not there?" I say mock-demurely, placing a dainty hand on my chest.

He smiles, albeit a tiny one, and looks at me amusedly across the table. "Yes, that's exactly it," he says jokingly. One more point against Martha's baseless claims.

A server brings our pizzas, and like clockwork, we eat a slice from our own, then exchange platters and enjoy a slice from the other's, repeating our little Pizza Dance until only one slice remains on my plate. I sit back in my wicker chair and hold my stomach, already bloated beyond relief.

"Eat it!" he practically yells.

"No!" I yell back.

"Eat it or I'll start telling another story from my childhood."

I blanche. "You wouldn't."

"When I was seven years old we had this cat named Archibald and this one time we let him out—"

"FINE, I'll eat it!" I extend an arm and lazily slide the slice off the platter, eating it from where I lounge back in my chair. "I feel like barfing. Happy now?"

"Turned my whole day around. Thank you."

It became a joke back when he worked at Common Ground—how anything and everything, no matter how insignificant, reminded him of some story from his twenty-three years of life. Parents, siblings, pets, any year of grade school, Danny always had something to say. Sometimes the stories made you double over in laughter, and sometimes they made your eyes gloss over from disinterest. Eventually we realized he was testing us, and that half of the time he would only go on until we asked him to stop. I was annoyed at all the wasted mental energy, but Martha thought it was a funny quirk.

"You're so welcome, Danny P."

He smiles the same contented smile he always does when I call him by his first name and last initial. I smile the same contented smile right back. The sun sets behind me, casting a glow over his amber eyes. When I realize I'm staring, I quickly look away, embarrassed.

But then, he was staring, too.

He offers to walk me home, and when I ask if it's because he's worried I'll topple over, he says it's because he parked by my building. I'm not surprised, since the pizza place's small parking lot only accommodates about one-third of its guests.

I groan upon rising from my chair, stuffed to the brim.

We take the paved trail that leads to the back of my building rather than the busy street, and I walk languidly, hunched over in a bid to make him feel sorry for forcing me to eat the last slice of pizza. He only laughs at my theatrics. "I hate you," I tell him, but I'm laughing too. I straighten to a normal posture and shove my hands in the pockets of my shorts, adopting a relaxed stroll beside him.

"So, what did *you* do with your day off?" he asks.

"I guess you could say I wrote?" I answer very, very convincingly.

"You wrote!" he exclaims, like it's the greatest thing he's ever heard.

I rear back, intimidated by his enthusiasm. "Just a little. Kind of aimlessly, too, like when you walk around Target just for the sake of walking around Target." He nods understandingly. "But…" My voice trails off.

"But what?" By now, we've reached the offshoot leading off to my building, and Danny leans against the fence opening, waiting for my answer.

I lean against the opposite end of the opening. "I don't know, I guess it just felt *good* to get lost in a story. It's been a while since I've lost track of time like I did today." Nothing like a few thousand words to make me this animated.

"That's awesome, Jane. Seriously."

"Thanks," I tell my feet.

"Are you ever going to let me read one of your stories?" he asks, and my head shoots back up.

He's been asking for years, almost every time I offhandedly mention anything about my casual writing. I always say no, that it's just something I do for myself. For fun. That I probably suck *"so you wouldn't want to read it, anyway."* I say a variation of the same now, just withholding the self-deprecation so Danny doesn't think I'm fishing for compliments.

If he ever had a chance of reading my story before, he certainly doesn't now. That chance jumped straight out the window and flew to Istanbul the second my two main characters showed up in the real world. Danny wouldn't see it that way. He'd see his former coworker, now certifiably crazy, writing fanfiction about two of her regular customers. I shudder inwardly at the thought.

"Fine. But if you ever change your mind…"

I angle my face up to look at him impatiently.

"… I'm ready and willing to be your biggest fan."

FOURTEEN

Martha opens the shop on Friday, so I don't roll in to work until ten minutes to seven, high on an extra hour of sleep.

There's only one customer seated in the shop, and Martha is very politely asking him to move so she can take down the anecdotal coffee artwork hanging above his head.

"What's going on?" I chuckle after clocking in and tying an apron around my waist.

"I got a call from this girl Izzie, wondering if she could hang some photos in the shop."

I blow air out of my cheeks. "Oh yeah, I gave her your card when she was here the other day."

"And? What do we think? Is she normal?"

I laugh. "Yeah, pretty normal. She called our aesthetic 'Parisian.'"

"Mmm," she muses. "I like that."

"I knew you would."

"Well, good, I'm glad she's normal. Because she'll be here in about twenty minutes."

My breath catches in my throat. Hysteria rises in my chest, and I'm tempted to whine, *I'm not ready for this!* In my head, I even stomp my foot.

But I'm a sort-of adult and I can handle this. I know, because I've done it before.

When she does arrive, I have to rush to the door to hold it open for her. I can't see her face over the pile of canvases in her arms, all of varying sizes.

I direct her to a four-top where she can set them down. She brushes her hands of invisible dirt once she's done so.

I give her a close-lipped smile, stare at her for just a beat too long, and return to the back of the counter even though I have no new customers.

It's annoying how beautiful she is, even though it's all my fault.

While slightly basing Izzie's looks off of my own (brown hair, olive skin), I improved upon all my own insecurities, projecting what I wished I had (straighter teeth, smaller hips) and it shows.

Some might even mistake us for sisters, which I guess would make me the taller, curvier one. *Couldn't have given her more flaws?*

Her eyes are dark but undeniably blue, whereas mine are, well, the only word that comes to mind is *muddled.* I suppose the official term is hazel, though I've always understood hazel to mean brown with green spots, or green with brown spots. I don't quite know what to call it when your eyes are sometimes both, and sometimes neither. Easily affected by the color of my shirt or the positioning of the sun.

Izzie and Martha get to work hanging up the photo canvases above some of the tables. I can't hear their conversation, but I do hear plenty of laughter.

I busy myself helping a new stream of customers and finding things to deep clean in between, like fishing out dusty pennies from deep underneath the counter.

At some point I go into the backroom and check my phone, only to find a text from Ben: *On my way for an Americano.* He sent it nearly ten minutes ago, which means he'll be walking in any minute.

Crap! Not while Izzie's here displaying her beautiful artwork for the world to see, outside of their frustrating work relationship! I can't let him see her.

I return to the front, senses heightened. I have to come up with something, fast.

"That frappe you made the other day was *so* good, by the way."

I snap to attention. Izzie's leaning across the counter, practically on my side. "Oh, thanks." Awkward silence. "Did you... want another one?"

She shakes her head. "Too early for that much sugary goodness. But I will take an iced white chocolate mocha!"

I don't point out that her alternative beverage is almost equally chalk full of sugary goodness. I nod and begin measuring out espresso grounds behind the machine.

The thought hits me while I'm combining the milk, syrup, espresso, and ice in a cocktail shaker.

Jane, no. Not again.

I strain the mixture into a plastic cup over fresh ice.

There are other ways.

I take the cup, now full, to the edge of the counter where Izzie waits, smiling.

Izzie doesn't deserve it. You'd feel so bad.

The door chimes behind me, sealing Izzie's fate.

Another flick of the wrist, and white chocolate raspberry mocha is dripping down Izzie's arm and the front of her shirt.

I gasp loudly, hopefully convincingly, swallowing the guilt rising in my throat. "Oh my God, I don't know what's wrong with me!" Technically true. Something *must* be wrong with me. "There's a bathroom over here where you can get washed up. I'll make you another one. On me!" I practically shove her toward the bathroom door. She lets out a laugh, and I don't have time to analyze if it's angry, astonished, or humored. She disappears behind the door, and when I hear the lock hatch, I spin back to the counter just in time to see Ben raising his eyebrows at me.

Oh God, please tell me he didn't see that. Please, please please.

"Heyyyy," I say in the least casual tone known to man. "What's up?"

"Maybe you didn't see my text," he says, and I sigh with relief. So he didn't see Izzie, or more importantly, what I did to her. He might get traumatic flashbacks to his own experience. "Americano, made with extra love, please."

I'm so focused on getting him out of here before Izzie returns from the bathroom that I almost miss what he said. Is he flirting with me? *Right now?*

I make his Americano at a record pace, weighing my options as I go. I can a) say something flirty back and risk getting into a long enough exchange with Ben that Izzie comes out and ruins everything, or b) I can send him out the door as soon as possible and hope to God that there will be an option to flirt later.

In the corner of my eye, I see a customer rise from her seat and try to bathroom door handle. Plan B it is, then.

"Well, here you go, extra love, extra EXTRA love! I'll see you later, let's hang later, have a great day!"

He looks at me strangely. You'd think he'd be used to my antics by now. "Okay, weirdo." He makes for the door while he talks. "I actually can't hang tonight, but—"

Behind me, I hear the bathroom door open, hear Izzie and the other woman exchange pleasantries as they scoot around each other.

"That's okay! No problem at all. Bye, Ben!"

I mentally will Ben out of the door, screaming inside my head like we're in a war movie. *Go! Go! Move out!*

He laughs and shakes his head, and, as if reading my mind, ducks out of the shop just as Izzie returns to the counter, holding her rinsed-out top away from her skin. I can see her lacey pink bra, but I don't care. I lean against the counter, out of breath. I expelled way too much energy on my shenanigans.

"I'm really sorry about your shirt," I say tiredly.

Izzie looks at me with sympathy in her eyes. Sympathy I don't deserve. "I've done worse."

I snort. "Oh yeah, like what?"

She smiles mischievously. "Like… spilling drinks on guys at bars to start a conversation."

Despite myself, I laugh loudly. Make that two crazy brunettes in Minneapolis intentionally ruining men's innerwear. "What ever happened to just saying 'hi'!"

She grins. "'Hi' is so old-fashioned. I prefer dramatic introductions. Dramatic entrances, too. Anything dramatic, really."

I wonder if she finds the drama in making eggs over easy, too, or if that's just a Me Thing.

"Okay, I think we're good," Martha says, plopping her little picture-hanging kit down. "Take a look and tell me what you think," she tells Izzie. "You, too," she says to me.

I follow Izzie to her five canvases, which Martha ended up arranging gallery wall-style. Izzie takes a cursory glance over the display before nodding in approval, only looking out for the set-up's appeal, whereas I look at the photos themselves.

They take my breath away.

Book Izzie's income comes from weddings and portraits, but her real passion lies in adventure. The gig projects merely serve to fund her travels, and she captures stories in a moment all across the world.

Real Izzie is no different.

The biggest of the canvases is from right here in Minneapolis, a shot of the historic Stone Arch Bridge from below. There are thousands of professional photos of the bridge, but this one is different. She specifically focused on the pedestrians peeking over the edge. One couple gazing into each other's eyes, a small boy waving (maybe at Izzie, maybe not) next to his father, who's angling his phone towards his son, taking a photo of his own, and an elderly man looking out over the skyline with such a contented expression that you can't help but wonder how long he's called this city home.

It's surprisingly intimate for a portrait of a bridge.

"This is amazing," I whisper in awe.

Izzie follows my gaze. "Ah. Had to show some hometown love, you know?"

I nod dumbly.

It's official: I wrote Izzie to be way cooler than me.

Now I understand why in my story, once Ben sees her other work outside of the book project, he can't get enough.

Izzie chewed on her lip as he flipped through her first professional portfolio. She'd never admit it, but she desperately wanted Ben's approval. If he teased her now, her pride would hurt. But that's always the risk in showing someone your art. You just have to choose people you trust.

He closed the folder, looking up at her with an open expression. "Can I see more?"

She raised her eyebrows. "Really?"

"Why wouldn't I be?"

"Aren't you bored?"

He laughed at her. "No, I want to see more."

"Okay," she said hesitantly. "What do you want to see next?"

I want to see more, too.

"What are you doing later?" Izzie suddenly asks.

"Huh?" I snap out of my reverie. "Oh. Uh…" *Well, I wanted to hang out with Ben, but now that's not happening,* I think, but refrain from voicing aloud. "Nothing. You?"

"I've got a wedding."

"On a Friday night?"

"Friday night weddings are the best!" she exclaims. "They don't last as long as weekend weddings and they're usually less maintenance."

"Huh." I let that mull over for a second.

"Anyway, wanna come?"

My head swivels to gawk at her. "Huh?"

"To the wedding. You can be my assistant." She's smiling like it's the most natural thing in the world to ask of someone she just met.

"You don't even know me," I argue. "I could be psycho."

She throws her head back and laughs. "There's nothing wrong with a little psycho. Besides, I know you're not. I have a good sense about people."

I doubt that—not when you can dislike someone like Ben at first sight.

I want to say no. I want to say, "Well how do I know *you're* not psycho?" but that would be untruthful. I know she's not. Besides, I already admitted to a lack of Friday night plans—she would know I'm lying if I say otherwise now.

And though I'm afraid to admit it, underneath it all, I'm drawn to Izzie, too. The curiosity is overwhelming. How does she compare to her literary version? Is she as well-traveled? Will she surprise me like Ben did?

"Come on!" she pleads. "All you'll have to do is hold the camera bag. It'll be fun! A few hours of work, an open bar, maybe some handsome, eligible out-of-towners, *if you know what I mean.*" She wiggles her eyebrows at the last part.

"Fine! I'll be there."

"Really?" she squeals, clasping her hands. Then in a flash she's looking at me scandalously. "It was the out-of-towners, wasn't it?"

I shake my head, laughing. "No!" I already have my eyes on a handsome, eligible man, but again, I don't tell Izzie this. "It was the open bar."

"A-ha!" She grins. "This'll be great. The wedding starts at five p.m. I usually wear some flowy black pants and a black blouse, just to set me apart from the guests, but you can wear whatever you want." She backtracks. "Well, not *whatever* you want. You can't wear jeans. You know what, maybe just wear all black, like me." She nods along to her own instructions. "Here, gimme your digits so I can text you the address." She hands me her cell, a fresh contact page already open, and I dutifully fill out the requisite information before handing it back, only mildly intimidated by her confidence. It's astonishing to see in real life.

Shortly after we hash out the details, she leaves with a new iced white chocolate mocha, off to meet Ben to work on her book, or maybe just to take more photos of bridges. Who knows? She didn't say.

Perhaps she will later, when I tag along as her plus-one.

"You're making friends left and right these days," Martha comments after Izzie's gone.

"I guess so." I smile. Laugh. Shake my head in wonder.

What a fascinating new development.

I already know the only black pants I own are of the denim variety, so after work I head to one of the suburban shopping malls for an acceptable outfit.

If I were a photographer's amateur assistant, what would I wear?

At the third store I visit, I find a flowy black jumpsuit in the sale section, so soft I could sleep in it, and even though it's a size too big, I snatch it up. I can throw a belt around the waist, but I can't beat the price, and on a barista's paygrade, I take any deal I can get.

Casey's locked up in her room on a work call when I get home, but Suze is on the couch, and when she sees my shopping bag she asks what I got, which leads to me trying it on for her, which leads to her lending me one of her belts, which leads to me explaining why I needed this outfit in the first place.

"What, so you're, like, friends now? I thought she was the competition." Suze's work sits unfinished on the coffee table, all her attention directed at me.

"She was—is. But I don't know, I think she wants to be friends."

"Is that what you want?"

I shrug. "Maybe?" I throw my legs over the back of the chair and let my hair fall from the seat cushion. "This is going to sound weird, but I think she feels a pull of some sort towards me. Ben, too."

"That does sound weird, but I guess it makes sense since you're their *creator* and all."

I tilt my chin up to look at her. She's looking back at me, upside down. "That sounds weird, too. I'm not a *god*."

"You got that right." She crinkles her nose, and I throw a pillow at her.

"Plus," I carry on as if she hadn't said anything. "I think I feel a pull towards them, too." I sigh. "It's hard to explain. I don't even know what I'm saying."

She hums a halfhearted reply, and I look to see she's gone back to work, no longer paying attention, still upside down.

I roll my eyes. Now that Suze's checked out of the conversation, I get up and move to my room, laying on my bed with the intention of taking a nap. I even set an alarm for when I'd need to get ready for the evening.

However, three hours later the alarm only alerts me that it's time to put my laptop away. I hit CTRL-S before even realizing I've written two-thousand words.

I'll have to review what I wrote later. There's no way it's all coherent after typing that much without stopping. For now, though, I need to freshen my makeup and do something with my hair.

Only when I pull up and park alongside several other cars does it dawn on me that I'm essentially crashing a wedding.

Well-dressed guests stream towards a large white barn, the ladies walking carefully so their heels don't get stuck in the dirt. Only a few people mill about outside the barn, where high-top tables are scattered around the building. Beyond, guests gather on a well-manicured lawn lit up by big, round string lights. Off to the side, rows of chairs and an aisle covered in flowers await its bride and groom. It'll look amazing once the sun sets.

I'm not sure I want to stick around that long, not with all these strangers. They'll know I don't belong right away.

I consider shooting Izzie an apology and high-tailing it out of here when someone knocks on my window. I startle and look up, wincing against the light to see Izzie peering inside. She gestures for me to come out, so I do.

Once again, we look like sisters, especially now that we're both in flowy black getups. We're both even rocking low ponytails, though I straightened my hair before pulling it back whereas Izzie left hers curly.

She has a fancy camera swung around her neck, the thick black strap working with her ensemble. She fiddles it as she greets me, and I wonder if it's a nervous tick before remembering Izzie doesn't get nervous. She'll strut in there like she belongs, which she does, while I squeeze her camera bag defensively to my chest, looking around wildly with paranoid, shifty eyes.

Izzie hands me her camera bag, as expected, and I follow her into the barn. I was expecting a country theme, but no, it's more rustic chic. Floral wallpaper, exposed wooden beams, a creaky wooden floor. There are even more string lights in here, especially surrounding the dancefloor.

A bar lines the far wall, and four bartenders busy themselves behind it, preparing for a reception that won't happen for hours. I wonder if Izzie was being serious when she said we'd be able to partake of the open bar. I hope so—I could really use something to loosen my nerves about being here in the first place.

Izzie goes to the back of the barn and up a set of stairs, me in tow. She knocks softly on a door on the landing, and a very feminine voice calls for us to come in.

The bride smiles at us when we walk in, then apologizes to the woman applying her lipstick, another shorter woman wearing a bridesmaid dress. In fact, all three of the bridesmaids are in here, as well as the bride's mother. Mirrors line each and every wall of the room, and there isn't one unoccupied space.

"This is Jane, my assistant," Izzie says as she focuses her lens.

"Hi, Jane," rings a chorus of female voices of varying pitch.

I smile tightly to be polite, even though everyone is too focused on their own faces to notice mine.

"I'm going to take some getting-ready shots, so just pretend I'm not here," Izzie starts circling the room. *Click, click, click.* The sound of purpose. While I stand here useless.

"Can somebody—I just need—arg," the mother of the bride grunts, reaching behind her shoulders to reach her dress zipper.

"Let me," I say when none of the bridesmaids pause their mascara-applying. I don't blame them—it's a high-risk business.

"Thank you." She smiles at me.

That's how I end up zipping and clipping, checking for blended foundation, plucking stray eyelashes from cheeks, and wiping setting powder from dresses.

By the time they're aisle-ready, I feel like I'm one of them. "Thank you, Jane!" "Thanks, Jane!" "You're the best, Jane!" They take turns saying as Izzie and I head out the door to get ready for them at the aisle, and I can't help but laugh.

Izzie laughs too, once the door is shut behind us. "I might have to edit you out of a few pictures."

We make to descend the stairs, but before we even take one step down, Izzie doubles over as if in pain.

"What's wrong?" I ask, worried she's injured. If she's injured, I might have to take the photos, and my only experience with photography is writing about it.

She grabs my arm and pulls me down to crouch beside her. "What is *he* doing here?"

"Who?" I ask, looking around wildly. As far as I can tell, it's only us and the bartenders inside the barn.

"*Him!*" She juts her finger in the direction of the bar tables outside the barn, and I have to narrow my eyes to see who she's looking at.

Of course.

My breath catches when I see him. He's the tallest person here, and he's wearing the crap out of his suit. "Ben?"

"Yes, Ben. You know him, right?" Her voice is frantic. I guess Real Izzie gets nervous, after all. "Did *you* know he'd be here?" she asks accusingly.

"No, he just said he was busy. Why are you freaking out?"

"I kind of... *raised my voice* at him earlier," she says meekly.

"While you were working on your book?" I ask, astonished. It's only been a couple days, for goodness' sake. How can tensions have boiled over already?

She cocks her head to the side. "You know about the book?"

"You know the bride's going to step out any minute now, right?" I ask purely so I don't have to explain that Ben talked about her. Don't want her getting any ideas.

"Crap, you're right." She stands, and so do I. "This'll be fun," she says sarcastically before huffing it down the stairs.

When I reach the base of the stairs, I freeze. What if my being here with Izzie somehow affects my relationship with Ben? What

154

if he doesn't want to spend time with me after he sees me in cahoots with his enemy?

Izzie doesn't notice that I've stopped following her, and I watch in horrified fascination as she marches straight towards Ben. His eyes darken when he sees her.

This is the moment I can run. Book it to my car, send a text to Izzie with some lie about an emergency, and hope Ben never finds out that I was ever here.

But there's something in Ben's eyes that prevents me from leaving. He's frowning at Izzie, yes, but I can tell he's riled up just at the sight of her. *Passion,* I realize. Izzie brings out the fire in Ben in a way no one else can, exactly how I wrote it—much to my dismay.

I can't leave. An open bar, romantic lighting… what if that passion translates to something other than hatred later? No, I have to stay and make sure it stays hatred. Which, granted, won't be easy since I'm friends with Ben and here with Izzie, but hey, points for trying.

Channeling my inner Izzie, I raise my chin and march right up to them.

"*Jane?*" Ben asks astonishingly when he sees me.

Whatever confidence I feigned flies out the window at his look of shock. "Hey," I say, voice tinny.

He looks between me and Izzie for a moment, and a little thrill runs through me when they eventually settle back on me. "What are you doing here?"

I gesture lamely in Izzie's direction. "She needed help, so…" I let my voice trail off, hoping he won't push it.

"What are *you* doing here?" he asks Izzie.

"Working," she says like it's obvious, which, it should be, what with the camera around her neck and all.

"Of course," he tells the sky, as if to say, *Just my luck.*

Suited men begin ushering guests to take their seats. Izzie wordlessly leaves us to take her position near the end of the aisle, leaving Ben and I in awkward silence.

"I didn't know you'd be here," I whisper, my voice apologetic. Then I realize I probably shouldn't make him think I have something to be sorry about. I'm about to say something else, perhaps "I just came for the open bar!" when he sighs, meets my eye again.

"You kicked me out before I could tell you."

I tilt my chin up to look at him, expecting an irritated expression, but he's smiling. "You're an odd one, Jane, you know that?"

I sigh, too. "Trust me, I know."

"Here," he gestures for me to follow him down the aisle, "you can sit with me."

I smile appreciatively, since the alternative is awkwardly standing at the back with nothing but a camera bag on my shoulder. I place it on the grass next to my feet.

Soft music begins playing, and we all crane our necks to see the first bridesmaid make her way down the lawn.

"Who do you know here, anyway?" I whisper, too curious to wait.

"The groom and I were roommates in college," he whispers back, close to my ear, and a shiver runs down my spine.

A roommate from college is news to me. I look at the groom, smiling next to three other men. All four men have the same brown skin. Brothers. I guess there's no point in asking why Ben isn't a groomsman.

Finally, the song changes, and I turn back in time to see the bride, arms locked with her father, weeping as she makes her way towards her soon-to-be husband. Izzie discreetly orbits around them to get the best shot.

Despite myself, I feel a tear welling.

Ben chuckles when he sees it. "Shut up," I hiss, dabbing at my eye. "I'm a sympathy crier."

He rolls his eyes before turning his attention back to the couple.

It's funny: I'm here with Izzie, but right now I can pretend that she isn't around. That I'm here as Ben's date, instead. At the very least, sitting here beside him makes me feel less like an outsider. I relax in my seat and watch the rest of the ceremony in peace.

Afterwards, Izzie grabs the wedding party and ushers them off to take more photos while the rest of us are led to a big banquet hall in the back of the barn that I hadn't noticed before.

"I should probably go wait in my car," I tell Ben, but before I can take a single step, he gently takes my arm in his hand.

"It's a buffet," he says. "No assigned seating, plenty of food."

That's enough to convince me. We choose a table with people Ben seems to know, another roommate from college and his girlfriend, as well as a couple from the bride's side he doesn't know. Introductions are exchanged, and I'm thankful for Ben for introducing me as his friend and *not* the bogus photographer's assistant that I actually am.

When the wedding party returns, Izzie forgoes eating to circulate the tables alongside the bride and groom as they greet their guests.

After snapping a candid photo of the bride hugging an elderly man, I catch a glimpse of something on Izzie's face. Is that… boredom?

I suppose that makes sense. She's a traveler, a restless spirit. Maybe her photography book will get her enough attention so she can spend more time doing what she loves, rather than what simply pays the bills.

I catch Ben watching her, too, and I wonder if he's thinking the exact same thing.

Is it too much to hope he's just thinking about how much he dislikes her?

When the dancing starts, and Izzie still hasn't given me any instruction (or even so much as glanced my way as long as I'm near Ben) I feel it's time for me to leave, but then Ben asks for two drinks at the bar and hands me one of them, and I figure another half hour at a wedding I don't belong at would be fine. I've made it through the ceremony and dinner, after all, and no one's accused me of being an imposter thus far.

I take a sip of my drink—red wine, of course—and mentally picture the guests in an uproar at my presence. *"You're not really a photographer's assistant,* are you?" The thought makes me giggle. No one here could care less.

"What are you snickering at?" Ben asks coyly.

"Oh, nothing," I say wistfully.

He shakes his head amusedly and takes a sip of wine. A flashback pops into my head: Ben on the dock, drinking from a plastic cup as he does now, looking at me like I'm a mystery to be solved, and I try to shake off the memory. When that doesn't work, I flag down the bartender and ask for a refill.

Ben excuses himself to use the bathroom, and only when I'm alone at the bar does Izzie approach. I wondered if she'd be mad, but she seems more relieved to get a moment of my time. She orders an old fashioned (again, way cooler than me) and leans against the bar. Her skin has a slight sheen to it, and I realize she's been taking photos from the middle of the dance floor. She fans herself. "Having fun?" she asks as she chews the boozy cherry, her tone neutral.

"Actually, yeah," I say in kind. "Ben's a good friend of mine."

She raises an eyebrow. "Just a friend?"

Is she asking because she's secretly attracted to him? What am I saying, of course she is. That much is canon. She may not know the reason behind her curiosity just yet, but I do. I purposefully look off to the side so it looks like I'm lying when I reply, "Yes, just a friend." It's a cheap move, I know, but what can I say? I'm weak.

She nods slowly, a mischievous smile on her lips. "Well, he's nice to *you*, anyway," she mutters under her breath.

I watch from across the room as Ben gets swept up in a conversation with the four brown men. He jostles the groom a little, and I smile to myself. Look at my Ben, making friends, all grown up.

Ew, Jane. You may have made *him, but you're not his mother.*

I make a face at my own train of thought, asking for yet another refill. The cups are relatively small, anyhow. Probably half the size of the ones Ben and I used on the dock. *Great, now we're thinking about the dock again.*

I turn to Izzie. "Why'd you yell at him today? Sorry, *raised your voice.*"

She laughs to herself. "Uhh…" She knocks back the rest of her cocktail. "It's stupid."

"Tell me," I push.

She turns her entire body to face me. "Okay, so you know about my book. Do you also know that he's my editor?"

I nod.

"Well, he started messing with the page layout of my photos, right, and I was all, 'You edit words! Stop trying to steal my job!' or something to that effect, and then he was all, 'It's my job, too, stop making things unnecessarily difficult,'" she lowers her voice for Ben's speaking line, and I laugh despite myself, "and then I may have said something harsh about his parents owning the company."

I stop laughing to gape at her. "Izzie, why would you do that?"

She throws her hands in the air. "How was I supposed to know it was a sensitive topic?"

I pinch the bridge of my nose. "And then what happened?"

161

"And then he clammed up and barely spoke to me for the rest of the day." She rings her hands. "I felt kinda bad about it."

I give her a pointed look. "Okay fine, I felt *really* bad about it. But he's been so uptight and grumpy ever since I met him at your coffee shop! I mean what is *up* with that?"

Go easy on him. He has a lot riding on your book's success. He's not as uptight as you think he is. And he's probably wildly attracted to you.

I voice none of my thoughts to Izzie. I can't afford to. Not when I stand to lose whatever it is I have with Ben. Still… I can't just say nothing.

"You have to apologize," I find myself saying.

"I know," she sighs.

She's watching Ben, too, and I wonder what she would be thinking and doing if I wasn't here. If I didn't exist. If this was just the story, and not the real world.

I would have them bump into each other. Someone would push them together to dance. Izzie would try to protest— *"But I have photos to take!"*—and the other person would say, *"Nonsense!"* and be on his or her merry way. Probably a *her.* Probably old and lovely. Ben would be secretly glad for the opportunity to hold Izzie in his arms, and she would learn something new about him and smile. It would be the beginning of a Something.

No. A kiss on the dock is a Something.

A slow song begins streaming through the loudspeakers, perfect for swaying, and I put my now empty cup on the bar and make my way across the dance floor to Ben. "Wanna dance?"

He smiles, gesturing for me to lead the way. When we're in the middle of the floor, I turn to him, suddenly shy. I don't know what I'm doing. I'm not this forward *ever.*

Thankfully, Ben does the work for me, taking my right hand in his and sliding the other around me. His hand rests on the small of my back, warm through the thin fabric of my jumpsuit. I put my free hand on his shoulder.

It's easy to follow his lead as we sway around to the rhythm, and I wonder if he'd catch me if I dropped dead from happiness.

"How did she die?" my parents would tearfully ask the coroner.

"Her heart was just too full," he would reply.

"Where do you go?" Ben asks, breaking me out of my reverie.

"Hmm?" I tilt my face up to look at him, blinking in surprise when I see how close our faces are.

"When you zone out like that, where do you go?" he repeats quietly. We're close enough that he doesn't have to raise his voice over the music.

I think about my story. I think about you.

"I don't know," I whisper.

His eyes search mine. They flick to my lips. I stop breathing.

My lips part ever so slightly, almost in expectation, and Ben leans in slowly.

Click.

Both our heads snap in the direction of the noise. Izzie's pointing her camera directly at us. *Click.*

I blink slowly, as if awoken from a trance. The music ends right then, sealing the deal. I step away from Ben.

What am I doing?

"I…have to go."

"What?" Ben and Izzie ask in unison.

I don't repeat myself. Instead, I shove Izzie's camera bag in her arms and flee in the opposite direction, out of the barn, into my car.

I see them in the rearview mirror, side by side, as they should be, while I drive off like a bat out of hell.

FIFTEEN

I have too much on my mind to sort my thoughts enough to write this evening's events, so I just lay on the couch in my jumpsuit (it really is quite comfortable).

Casey and Suze have long since gone to bed, and I don't bother switching on any lamps. Sleep will come eventually, I'm sure. For now, I can't stop mentally debating if I'm the main female lead or the second.

I still haven't figured it out when my phone buzzes on the floor around one a.m.

Are you up? Izzie asks.

I put the phone back down without answering. Then, two seconds later, I pick it back up. *Yeah.*

She responds right away. *Can we talk?*

Now?

I'm outside.

I rise from the couch to peek out the front window. Sure enough, Izzie's sitting on the one picnic table in our little courtyard. I grab my keys and head outside.

"How do you know where I live?"

Izzie puts her phone away when she seems me. "Ben told me."

"You guys talked about me?" I sit on the table next to her, resting my feet on the bench.

She looks at me like I'm an idiot. "No, after you ran away for no reason, we decided to swap political views—*yes, we talked about you.*"

I ignore her sarcasm, even though it's completely warranted. "What did he say?"

"I think he was more confused than anything else. He wanted to come talk to you, but I asked if I could, first."

I wait for disappointment to sink in at the idea that I could be here with Ben in the middle of the night rather than Izzie, but it never comes.

"I apologized to him, too. About what I said." She looks at me. "Thought you might want to know."

I smile. So does Izzie.

"So do you want to tell me what happened back there, or do I have to guess?"

I tap my lips thoughtfully. "Hmm… guess."

She shoots me an impatient look. "Fine."

Am I really about to do this?

She looks at me expectantly.

I can't do this.

"I'm just… trying to figure some things out."

She sighs. "Vague, but I'll let it slide. For now."

Neither of us say anything for a minute, but it isn't uncomfortable. Rather, it feels like being with an old friend.

"I'm a writer," I blurt unexpectedly, and even Izzie startles.

"Okay," she says slowly.

"I write about people. People who fall in love."

She's clearly trying her best to follow along. "Like, romance?"

"I guess? Anyway, I kind of abandoned this one story for years because I lost steam, or got writer's block or something, I don't know. But lately, I've started writing again, and it feels… great. Like I'm myself again." *Why am I telling her all of this?*

To Izzie's credit, she doesn't look at me like I'm a whack job. In fact, she nods along understandingly. "I totally get it. I never feel more like myself than when I'm behind the camera in some foreign country, but trust me, photographer's block is a thing."

"Really?" I ask, incredulous.

"Oh, yeah. Sometimes I'm surrounded by so much beauty that none of it stands out in a special way. And sometimes I'll try for hours to get the shot I picture in my head, only to just give up."

I rest my elbows on my knees and tilt my head to the side thoughtfully. "What do you do when that happens?"

She gives me a small smile. "I go for a walk. No camera, no phone, just me."

"And that works?" I can't mask the skepticism in my voice.

She laughs. "Not all the time, but it helps me regain focus. Forces me to look at the world without filtering it through a lens—literally *and* figuratively."

I scoff. "A walk," I repeat.

"A nice, long one." She stretches out each word for emphasis.

"Huh." I mull over her words for a bit.

"Anyway, I think it's super cool that you're a writer." She looks off, deep in thought. "It's not easy when the thing you love to do isn't exactly the most stable choice." She turns to me, grinning wickedly. "But it *does* make us more interesting."

I've always known that my life goes against the grain. I never went to college, I don't work full time, I sleep in a *dining room,* and a fun time for me involves making up stories in my head. But I never once thought of my life as being different *in a good way.*

Not until now, that is.

"You're pretty cool, yourself, Izzie," I say, and mean it. I look down at my lap. "I can see why Ben likes you," I add softly, but deliberately.

Her head swivels around the gawk at me. "Are you crazy? He hates me. I hate him!"

An amused laugh escapes me. "It's not funny!" she yells, and I shush her when an apartment light flicks on above us. "*It's not funny*," she repeats, this time as a whisper-scream.

"Trust me, I know it doesn't seem like it now, but Ben has a lot going on beneath the surface. And he likes you more than even he knows."

She looks pained. "How could you possibly know that? Has he said something?"

"No. I just know. I can't explain why."

She buries her face in her hands. I suspect it has something to do with the hidden smile tugging at her lips. I indulge in a knowing smile of my own.

Someday, when Ben's heart slowly melts in favor of Izzie, I may regret ever telling Izzie how he feels. But right now, I only feel like I'm using my powers for good. This moment with Izzie makes the confession feel worthwhile.

"You must really know him," Izzie mumbles into her hands.

"You have no idea."

* * *

I wake up relatively early on Saturday but lounge around in my bed most of the morning, half wasting time on my phone and half reading through my old story to find the moment Ben and Izzie's opinions begin to change about each other.

Oddly enough, the moment takes place at a coffee shop, one not unlike Common Ground. Ben and Izzie sit across from each other at four-top by the front window, a spread of the first draft, now coming along more smoothly, in front of them.

For once, Izzie didn't think Ben was being condescending. He was listening to her opinions, really *listening, and applying her suggestions to the layout in front of him.*

Ben, for his part, knew the final layout would be a product of the design team, but he also understood that these photos were Izzie's and Izzie's alone, and if a certain combination made sense in her mind, then she deserved the opportunity to see it through. Patience was a virtue difficult to master, but Ben was nothing if not an excellent learner.

Izzie munched absentmindedly on a peanut butter cookie— her favorite—as she sorted through the edits Ben had made to her photo blurbs. She no longer complained about the edits. Writing was never Izzie's strong point, but Ben was right when he said short descriptions and stories behind the photos would make the book more interesting.

When she reached for another piece, her hand met only crumbs on a cold, ceramic plate. She glanced down to see that the cookie was, in fact, gone.

Crunch.

She snapped her head up, shooting Ben a look of betrayal. Technically he paid for it, yes, but it was Izzie's *cookie.*

Ben held up the last coveted piece—a good one, too. Not too soft, not too crunchy.

"Give. That. Back."

"Work late with me tonight," *he bargains.*

It was clear from the start that they had wildly opposing work ethics, and Izzie wasn't about to let a Cookie Terrorist make her work overtime on a Friday night.

"Weekends are too fun to waste on a coffee book table," *she argued, reaching across the table for the cookie. Ben reared back defensively.*

"Too bad." *He grinned, eating the rest of the cookie while Izzie watched on in despair. He brushed the crumbs off his fingers, an annoying smirk plastered on his face. No remorse.*

"I can't believe you just did that."

He held up his hands in a "what can I say?" *gesture. Izzie lifted her mug to her lips, glaring at him over the top of it while trying to enjoy a now un-partnered beverage.*

"It's not just a coffee book table," *Ben suddenly said.*

171

Izzie looked up at him, no longer glaring. "What?"

"It's more than that," he continued. "Your heart and soul is evident in every one of these pictures. Our readers will see that."

Izzie could hardly believe it. She thought her ears must be playing tricks on her. Ben was already back to work, clicking around at the layout on his laptop screen, and she could just about convince herself that she misheard him.

But he did say it. And it was one of the kindest things anyone has ever said about her work. She never dreamed it would come from Benjamin King.

I'm just thinking about adding in the thing about Ben's promotion hinging on the success of Izzie's book when I get a text from the man himself, asking if he could come over, and I suddenly remember Izzie mentioning Ben had wanted to talk to me the night before.

I text him back to let him know I'm free all day, figuring we'll meet up later in the evening, but when he responds back saying he's on his way *now,* I shoot up from the bed and grab clean clothes like a madwoman, cranking open the window to air out my stale room and making a mad dash to the bathroom for a shower. My hair is at the threshold of "could pass for another day without washing, but probably not a good idea when someone as attractive as Ben is on their way over," so I shampoo and condition like my life depends on it.

I don't have time to dry it, or even to slap on so much as mascara, so I tie my wet hair up into a drippy bun and brush out my eyebrows so I at least look somewhat put together.

When I step out of the bathroom, I nearly run into Casey, on her way to her own room. She points behind her towards the living room. "Ben's here, I let him in."

"Thanks!" I tell her before entering the living room. Ben's not here.

I scoot around my folding wall to come upon Ben, standing in the middle of my room, holding my laptop.

Whoosh. All the blood drains from my head.

He turns to me slowly, his face a heartbreaking mixture of confusion, anger, and betrayal. "What is this, Jane?" His voice is low, shaking with suppressed emotion. I shrink back against it.

My knees wobble, and I grasp the wall for support. This time I might really pass out, but not from a full heart. I try to open my mouth, but no words come out. My mouth bobs stupidly, like a fish out of water.

"Have you been writing about me? About... *Isabel?*" He tosses my laptop down on my comforter in disgust, and I flinch as if he threw it at me. "Have you been watching us?"

"I..." My voice is pathetically weak. I search for something—anything—to diffuse the situation, fast. "I..."

His mouth pushes into a firm line, like it's difficult for him to even look at me.

Suddenly he charges past me, towards the door.

"Wait, Ben, I can explain!" I cry, but it's too late. I waited too long. He ignores my plea, throwing the front door open and storming out.

I stand there in the middle of the living room, my mouth open in shock. *What just happened? What just happened?* I keep asking myself.

Casey and Suze poke their heads out of their rooms, approaching slowly when I don't respond to their inquiries.

I feel a hand on my shoulder—Suze, gently asking if I'm alright.

I can't form the words to tell them that I'm not. All I can manage is to burst into tears.

SIXTEEN

Ben refuses to answer my calls and texts, of which there are many. I don't try to make sense the situation over text, I only stress that what he saw must be explained in person. Still, nothing.

Every day at work, I hold out hope that he'll put aside his anger for an Americano. My heart pounds every time the bell above the door chimes, but it's never him.

Casey and Suze tell me to give it time, but when a week passes with no word, I begin to lose all hope. Innumerable thoughts and emotions run through my mind as a near-constant stream of text, but I haven't so much as looked at my laptop since Ben found the story, let alone written anything down. I can't seem to scrounge up the desire nor the energy to write even a single word.

Izzie visited the shop only twice, both short visits since I could barely meet her eye. We exchanged enough conversation to establish that she's still in the dark about the story. On the one hand, it's incredibly relieving that Ben hasn't said anything; on the other, it could be indifference that's preventing him from telling Izzie, and if that be the case, I may simply never see him again.

Martha orbits around me the following Friday morning, glancing at me every so often in the corner of her eye. "Jane, are you doing alright?" she eventually asks. "You haven't been yourself this week."

I muster a smile. "I'm just tired." It's a poor excuse and we both know it, so I elaborate: "I've been having a hard time sleeping." That much is true—I toss and turn for hours each night, replaying the scene in my room over and over again, like a horror movie. *"What is this, Jane?"* Rewind, press play. *"What is this, Jane?"*

Martha narrows her eyes at me suspiciously, but eventually chooses to let it go. "Well, I'm here to talk if you need to."

The smile I give her is real. Martha's always been more than just a good boss.

Behind me, the door chimes, and Martha's face lights up in recognition. For a split second I can't breathe, until Martha says, "Lookin' good!" Surely, she wouldn't be saying that to Ben.

I turn around to see Danny wearing a suit, much nicer than his usual business casual getup. Navy blue suit, floral skinny tie—a bold choice, but it works on him. His hair, normally parted casually and constantly falling into his forehead, is pushed back.

He looks good.

"Morning, Martha," he beams. Then, without even taking his eyes off of her: "Jane, please stop objectifying me."

Martha chuckles behind me before excusing herself to make a phone call.

"What's all this?" I gesture vaguely in front of his chest.

"I've got a marketing pitch today," he explains, looking down at himself. "Had to dress the part."

I nod quietly, trying not to stare and failing miserably. "You look…" My voice trails off, and it takes all in my power not to slap myself across the forehead. "Nice tie."

He watches me closely, a smile playing on his lips. "You like it?"

I nod again. A delighted grin breaks out across his face. I get to work making his latte, suddenly hyperaware of my bare face. Why did I let my misery affect my daily routine? Why?

"So listen," Danny says when I hand him his drink at the other end of the bar. "If the pitch goes well, the higher-ups said they'd take the team out to celebrate. Would you, maybe, want to be my plus-one?"

"'Maybe'?" I ask playfully.

He rolls his eyes. "Look, it's free food, probably at some fancy restaurant, and I'm sick of being the only one without a date. You in?"

I open my mouth to say yes, I'll be his date, when the door chimes and Ben walks in. The words freeze in my mouth when he spots me immediately.

Ben's eyes sweep across me, then Danny, eventually settling on some unknown spot behind the counter while he waits for me to finish up. Judging from his stance, I know he won't wait long.

I turn back to Danny only to find his entire expression has changed. My breath catches in my throat. "You know what?" He picks up his latte. "Never mind."

He turns on his heel and exits the coffee shop, leaving me stunned.

I turn slowly to look at Ben, then the door. In a flash, I'm sprinting towards the door without glancing back. I can only hope Ben will wait for me, but right now, I couldn't care less.

I spot Danny's back as he walks down the sidewalk towards his car, and I start after him. "Danny!" I call, but he doesn't stop. I get closer. "Danny!" Still nothing.

"Danny P.!" I cry. Finally he stops, right in front of his car.

He turns around, looking at me impatiently. "I have to get to work," he says coolly, and it's wrong, all wrong. I've never seen him like this.

"What—what just happened?" I ask incredulously.

"Nothing," he says, making it overtly obvious that it's anything but.

"Danny…" I say again, but he shakes his head.

"I have to go," he says without looking at me. There's nothing I can do but watch him climb into his car and drive off.

I wait, dejected, until his car disappears around a corner before turning to walk back to the coffee shop, passing ANTIQUES on my way.

That's when I notice the rows and rows of empty shelves inside the dark shop. There's a "Closed" sign on the door. "Closed." That's it. So much finality in one little word.

I feel as if I've lost a bet.

Then, I realize it's just loss.

By some miracle, Ben hasn't left. He's now seated at a table near the back with a mug in front of him.

Martha's standing behind the counter with knowing eyes. "Why don't you take fifteen," she says, gesturing with her head in Ben's general direction. She hands me a cup of coffee to seal the deal.

Ben looks up when I take a seat across from him, keeping my hands wrapped around my mug on the table. The warmth provides a sense of security, even if it is a false one.

"Everything okay?" he asks, and I know he's not asking in a general sense. Maybe he feels bad.

I shake my head. "I don't want to talk about Danny."

He nods, but doesn't say anything else. It dawns on me that he's giving me the floor. Waiting for me to start first. The proverbial ball in my court.

I take a deep breath. And then I tell him a story... about a story.

"Around three years ago, I started writing a book. The leading man's name was Benjamin King..."

SEVENTEEN

B en's face goes through several metamorphoses during my explanation, ranging from understandable disbelief to outright shock, but he never denies the impossible truth: somehow, I wrote him and Izzie into existence.

"Hold on," Ben interjects for the millionth time. "If you're not the leading lady, then who is?"

I look at him pointedly.

His eyebrows rise in surprise. "*Isabel?*"

I scoff. "You're the only one who calls her that, Ben."

"I know, it's because she hates it." He's speaking very earnestly, as if he has to convince *me*. "She hates me. I hate her!"

I look at him sympathetically. "Yeah, it's kind of an 'enemies-to-lovers' thing."

He sits back in his chair, letting it all sink in. "I'm going insane," he tells no one in particular.

"Now you know how I felt when you first walked in here."

"I mean, have I existed all this time?" he continues as if I never said anything. "Or did you write me into existence? Or is this just some crazy coincidence where you just *happened* to write a character with my name, my face, my employment—"

"You're asking all the same questions I did, Benny Boy."

"This can't be real."

"I'm still not 100% convinced that it is, quite frankly."

He's silent for a long time, processing in twenty minutes what I had two months to digest.

Finally, he meets my gaze. "What do we do now?"

I frown. "What do you mean?"

"I mean, do we stay friends? Do we pretend not to know each other; move on with our lives?"

"Oh." I hadn't even thought about what we would do if he ever found out. "I don't know."

"What do you want?" he asks. "You're the one in charge, anyway."

I snort, I can't help it. Ben King in all his editorial glory just told his barista that *she's* the one calling the shots. Like I'm a high-ranking official or something.

"Jane?"

"Sorry, still thinking."

I may never know how any of this came to be, but one thig is for certain: I've been able to get to know my characters in a way no writer ever has before. I mean, these people have been in my head for years. It's like we've always been…

"Friends," I finish aloud. "I think we should be friends."

Ben nods. "Friends. Okay, yeah."

We let this settle between us.

Really, we're agreeing to continue being friends. Friends who shared one hazy holiday kiss, yes, but friends, nonetheless. The memory makes me smile. Seems so inconsequential now.

Ben's resorted to zoning out like it's an Olympic sport.

"Ben?" I ask. "Ben, you okay?"

"I think I'm having an existential crisis." He looks up at the ceiling thoughtfully. "In fact, I'm sure of it."

I pat his shoulder awkwardly. "There, there."

He starts laughing then, quietly at first but growing in hysteria, and it attracts the attention from a few other people— including Martha, who points at her watch. I've gone way past my fifteen minutes.

"Listen, I've got to get back to work, but um, Ben?" I wait for him to stop laughing. He rubs his hand over his mouth and looks up at me. "I don't know how any of this happened, but I do know one thing for sure."

With those dark eyes I know so very well, he watches me expectantly.

"You're as real a person as anyone else."

He meets my eye and smiles.

My phone buzzes later when I'm lounging around the living room with Casey and Suze, and I grab it excitedly thinking it might be Danny replying to the rather desperate "*How did your pitch go?*" text I sent earlier. Instead, it's Izzie asking if we can meet up.

I put my phone down. "Guys, Izzie wants to talk."

I've just spent the better part of the evening catching them up on the day's events. There's a general sense of relief in the room now that Ben is no longer avoiding me, but I still can't seem to find the motivation to return to my laptop.

"Do you think Ben told her?" Suze asks.

"I don't know," I answer.

"Did you ask him not to?" Casey asks.

"No. Should I have?"

She shrugs. "Guess you'll find out."

It's twilight out, and I don't bother changing out of my loungewear before meeting Izzie at the nearest lake to our apartment. It takes me five minutes to reach the lake and another ten to find Izzie halfway around it, sitting crisscross on a dock bench overlooking the water.

"Hey," I say hesitantly, just in case Ben did tell her about the story.

"Hey," she smiles back. I have to imagine she wouldn't be smiling if she were going through the same existential crisis Ben did this morning.

I plop down next to her. "What's up?"

"Funny thing," she starts. "Ben was acting weird today—well, weirder than normal—but when I asked what was up with him, he said to talk to *you*. Care to explain?"

"He really didn't say anything?" She shakes her head. "Nothing at all?"

"Jane, what's going on?"

I sigh. Evidently, this doesn't get easier with practice. "You're a character in a book I started three years ago and I don't know how you exist. Also, Ben is your romantic interest."

She chuckles. "Yeah, okay." When I remain silent, her eyes bulge. "*Nah...*"

I explain everything I did to Ben, listing all the facts I know about her life—way too many for her to even try denying my story.

"Is that all?" she laughs when I'm done talking.

"You're not upset?"

"Why would I be? I mean, it is what it is, right?"

"I guess…"

She keeps laughing. "Should I call you '*mom*'?"

I start laughing too. "You're handling it way better than Ben did."

She laughs harder. "Oh my God, *Ben*. That explains why he couldn't even look me in the eye today." She clutches her stomach. "I'm his betrothed!"

"Hey, it's no guarantee," I warn. "I never got that far in the story."

She shakes her head in amazement. "What made you stop writing it?"

I inhale. "I'm not sure, exactly. I think I just lost momentum. There was nothing driving the plot forward."

"And now?" she asks, gesturing to herself.

"It's evolved," I admit for the first time out loud. "I'm in it now, too."

She nods. "Makes sense." She rises from her seat. "Well, *mom,* I hate to cut it short, but Ben asked me to call him after I was done talking to you."

"Did he now?" I reply, tongue in cheek.

She shrugs defensively. "Hey, maybe he wants to tell me it's never gonna happen between us."

"I seriously doubt that."

She rolls her eyes. "Oh! I almost forgot." She reaches into her back pocket and produces a small rectangular photo. She hands it to me before she turns to leave.

"Hey, Izzie?"

She stops, turns back around to me, eyebrows raised.

"I'm glad we met."

She smiles. "Me, too."

With that, she's off to meet the leading man—*her* leading man.

I look down at the photo in my hand. It's of Ben and I slow dancing at the wedding, before we turned towards the camera. It's pretty obvious what was about to happen. I chuckle quietly, picturing Izzie deliberately preventing a kiss from happening. She can try to hide it all she wants, but she cares for Ben. I made absolutely sure of that.

I sit for a while in the dark, pondering over everything: Benjamin King, Isabel Archer, Danny P., Common Ground, Casey, Suze, Martha, ANTIQUES, "Untitled," "Americano," "Untitled II."

Suddenly, perhaps for the first time in my entire life, I know exactly what do to next.

EIGHTEEN

I change the story. Or maybe it changed itself.

I'm now a bona fide character—the *main* character. Every event, every verbal exchange I can remember from the moment Ben stepped foot in Common Ground and onward flows out of me like a beam, powering my fingertips to keep cracking at the keyboard. It helps that most of it was already documented in "Untitled II."

I take the events of the last two months, the last three years, and I run with it. Sprint, more like. I only stop writing to go to work, and even then, I bring my laptop with me and park myself at a table to write the instant I clock out.

I barely eat, barely remember to drink water, haven't had a real conversation with Casey and Suze in two weeks, and my legs are in serious need of a shave. I live and breathe this new story. Nothing else matters.

It goes beyond Ben, Izzie, and me. I make characters for Casey and Suze, Martha, even Danny P. *Especially* Danny P.

It isn't all pretty. Or cohesive. Sometimes I get blocked, or forget a detail, but when that happens, I do what Izzie told me to do and I go for a stroll. No phone, no earphones, just a silent jaunt around the lake to clear my head. Usually, it works.

I don't let the original story go to waste, either. I select the best scenes—the funny and the poignant—and weave them through the new story, essentially becoming both the main character and the main conflict—the conflict the other story had always lacked. Who knew it would turn out to be me?

I write, and write, and write.

Finally, one day, I reach the last chapter. The curser and I blink at each other.

I don't know how the story ends.

But I think I know who can help me.

NINETEEN

"Hey, stranger," Danny says warmly when I approach him outside of the coffee shop after work. My chest fills with relief. I haven't received so much as a single text from him since he stormed out of Common Ground. I wasn't even convinced he would show up today.

I look sideways at him. "You're not still mad at me?"

He smiles meekly and looks down at the ground. "Ah, no. Come to think of it, I don't even know what I was mad about." He meets my eye, his filled with apology. "Sorry."

I shake my head furiously. "Don't be sorry. *I'm* sorry. For not realizing sooner..."

His eyebrow twitches, and he watches me closely. Searching my face. I fidget under his gaze.

"I wrote a book," is what I manage to say.

"What about?"

"My life." I look to the side. "Sort of."

"Yeah?" He smiles lopsidedly. "How does it end?"

"That depends," I say, moving closer.

"On?" he asks amusedly, but he's moving closer, too.

People always ask me why I call him Danny P.

It's because my first day at the coffee shop, during a round of requisite introductions, he leaned back against the counter and said, "Hey, what's up, I'm Danny P." in the most laidback voice I've ever heard, as if he were a surfer dude and not a collegiate Midwesterner thousands of miles from the nearest body of saltwater. The name somehow immortalized itself in my mind. It just stuck.

Though I was always too scared to admit it, Danny P. stuck, too.

I'm not scared anymore.

"On you," I say with finality. We're so close now, I have to look up to meet his eye. "I like you so much, Danny P."

A grin spreads slowly across his face. He brushes his finger lightly across my cheek. I wait for his lips to meet mine.

Instead, he tips his head back and yells, "*Finally!*"

I frown. "Huh?"

"Took you long enough."

"Okay, I'm lost." I try to remove his hand from my face, but he grabs my hand in his and pulls me closer.

"Why do you think I have such a good memory?" he asks patiently, willing me to understand something not yet clear.

He remembers the names of my roommates, the young marriage life of Manda and Cam, my writing. He doesn't go to Common Ground on my day off. He invites me out all the time. He hasn't dated anyone since he quit the shop.

The realization washes over me. He must see it on my face, because he leans close. "It's because it's *you*, Jane. Your life."

It was always going to be Danny P. Not a near miss, but my perfectly imperfect Leading Man.

I throw my arms around his neck and kiss him first. He reacts swiftly, wrapping his arms around my waist and pulling me closer. I don't know how long we stand there. All I know is that we make up for lost time.

When we finally pull apart, I take an unsteady step away from him. "I gotta go."

"What?" he exclaims. "*Now?*"

"I told you, I have a book to finish."

He shakes his head in disbelief, but he's laughing. "I guess this is what I get for dating a writer."

I grin and kiss him again. Then I dash off to finish the story.

I smile the entire time I write the scene. It makes perfect sense. Looking back, I should've known this is how it would end.

CTRL-S. I lean back in my seat.

So this is it. Rather anticlimactic.

There are edits to be made, proofreading to attend to, but for now, I close my laptop and join Casey and Suze in the living room for the first time in weeks.

"Well, look who it is!" Casey says.

All of my time has been spent in my room, working on the story. I realize I've missed my roommates.

"How's the writing coming along?" Suze asks.

I smile down at my lap. "I finished it."

"What!" they both shriek.

"It still needs a lot of work, but..." I take turns looking at both of them. "Will you be my first readers?"

"Of course!" Casey says at the same time Suze says, "Hell, yeah!"

I laugh. "I love you guys."

It's a rare moment of gushiness, but I can tell they're touched.

I sigh, adopting my usual position of sitting upside down in the chair. "I wonder what Izzie and Ben will think."

"Right," Casey laughs, shaking her head.

A laugh escapes me. "What do you think they've been up to?" I ask neither of them in particular.

Suze smiles. "Only you know."

"Yeah, right." I kick my leg against the wall. "I've been holed up for weeks. They could be married by now, for all I know."

My words are met with silence. I sit up, frowning. I look back and forth between Casey and Suze, who stare at me with matching confused expressions on their faces. "What?" I ask, suddenly fearful.

Casey and Suze exchange a look, adding to hysteria bubbling inside my chest.

"Jane…" Suze says.

Casey finishes for her. "What are you talking about?"

TWENTY

They're gone.

Sometime between saying goodbye to Izzie on the dock and now, she and Ben just vanished. As if they never even existed in the first place—which, I suppose, they never really did.

No one remembers them. Casey and Suze even remember events differently, such as the cabin trip. And now it makes sense why Danny couldn't remember what he was upset about. Only my memory holds the truth.

Or maybe I'm just crazy. Maybe I've had this story idea buried in my mind longer than I thought. Perhaps it was a coping mechanism to my years-long writer's block—Izzie and Ben's story was stalled, so I brought them into mine. Made it real in my mind.

195

I can't find the photo Izzie took of Ben and me anywhere. For all I know, it never existed, either. Their contacts, too, have been wiped from my phone. All our text exchanges, every piece of evidence proving they were ever here, *gone.*

Suddenly, my final chapter feels incomplete. None of this feels right. They can't just leave, not without saying goodbye. It can't end like this.

I keep asking myself what Izzie would do in this situation. She would probably buy a plane ticket. I begin looking up flight deals, bookmarking the most promising. Then I research creative writing courses in Minneapolis. Then I find myself Googling terms like "Self-Publishing."

Of course, I have to finish the book before I can even think about publishing it. But how can I write a proper farewell when I never got one myself?

On Tuesday, my closing shift, Danny comes in and kisses me across the counter, leaving Martha positively stunned. "What—when—how?"

She couldn't be happier for us.

I sit across Danny while he eats his avocado toast, resting my head on folded arms. Something dawns on me.

"Hey," I say, sitting up. "Do you remember that guy I spilled coffee all over?" I hold my breath.

"Meet-Cute Guy?" he asks casually, and I crumble over the table in relief.

I'm not crazy. They were here, they were real. *But then why didn't they say goodbye?*

"Haven't seen him since. Guess you scared him off," he laughs.

I laugh too, still full of relief. "I guess so."

Gazing up at Danny, I remind myself what I do have. My roommates, my new boyfriend, Martha, Common Ground.

I don't know what my future looks like, and that's okay. Maybe I'll take a writing course, maybe I'll do some traveling. Either way, my roots are here. Besides, I can't yet imagine a life without Common Ground or Martha.

I walk Danny to his car, hands locked and swinging comfortably, until we pass the gutted shop that was once ANTIQUES. We stop in front of it, and by some unspoken agreement hold a silent vigil.

"I'm going to miss them," I whisper. "I mean, *it.*"

He squeezes my hand. "Me, too."

Later, when I'm alone in my room, I think about Ben and Izzie.

Slowly, I open the document, and I start to write.

"Endings always make me so sad," Izzie sighed.

Ben took her hand in his. They exchanged a smile.

I already missed them so much. "What will I do without you?" *I asked tearfully.*

A stray tear plops on the keyboard, and I wipe at my cheek.

"You'll do what you always do," Ben told me. "You'll write."

"Write," I repeated quietly. I nodded resolutely.

Izzie smiled. "She's ready."

I lay back on my bed, watching the farewell unfold so vividly in my mind that if I didn't know better, I never would've guessed I made the whole thing up. I know they wouldn't mind.

It was all a fiction, these words of mine.

Acknowledgments

Reader, I thank you. Writing a book was oodles and oodles of fun, and kept me busy during a not-so-fun time of human history (*cough* *global pandemic* *cough*). Countless rounds of edits, formatting, and design? A few oodles less fun. But I can easily say the fact that you're holding this in your hands right now makes it all worthwhile. Even the formatting. Truly.

Now, is it too cheesy to thank my family and friends for believing in me even when I didn't? Well, I'm doing it anyway.

You know who you are.

About the Author

Elizabeth Kenyon is many things: Proofreader, barista, former occasional trash-hauler (don't ask), reader, and mood-based writer. Growing up, she read every book she could get her hands on, and it was this lifelong love of fiction that inspired Elizabeth to begin writing her own stories at a very young age—abandoning each and every one of them when a newer, shinier idea came along.

Now, she lives, works, and reads in Minnesota, writing only when the never-ending stream of words in her brain results in something worthwhile. If only that would stop happening in the dead of night.

Made in the USA
Monee, IL
14 August 2020

38291802R00121